P9-BAU-755

Santa Paws
to the Rescue

by Nicholas Edwards

AN
APPLE
PAPERBACK

SCHOLASTIC INC.

New York   Toronto   London   Auckland   Sydney
Mexico City   New Delhi   Hong Kong

For Buddy, my pal
and
For Maggie, sweet as can be

If you purchased this book without a cover, you should be aware that this book is stolen property. It was reported as "unsold and destroyed" to the publisher, and neither the author nor the publisher has received any payment for this "stripped book."

No part of this publication may be reproduced in whole or in part, or stored in a retrieval system, or transmitted in any form or by any means, electronic, mechanical, photocopying, recording, or otherwise, without written permission of the publisher. For information regarding permission, write to Scholastic Inc., Attention: Permissions Department, 555 Broadway, New York, NY 10012.

ISBN 0-439-20849-1

Copyright © 2000 by Ellen Emerson White. All rights reserved. Published by Scholastic Inc. SCHOLASTIC, APPLE PAPERBACKS, and associated logos are trademarks and/or registered trademarks of Scholastic Inc.

12 11 10 9 8 7 6   2 3 4 5/0

Printed in the U.S.A.   40

First Scholastic printing, November 2000

1

The dog was having a great day. His three main requirements for this were lots of food, naps, and fun. Just now, when he was sleeping in front of the fireplace, he even had a dream about playing a game which involved hunting for hidden Milk-Bones! Of course, his whole family was in his dream, too, all of them smiling and helping him find the biscuits. He *loved* the Callahans more than anything, and felt very lucky that he was their dog. Unfortunately, he woke up from his nap when his cat friend, Abigail, jumped down on top of him from the mantlepiece. She pretended that it was an accident, but the dog was pretty sure she had been *aiming* for him. That was still okay, though, because it gave him a great excuse to chase her.

The dog was a little off balance as he jumped up to run after her, and he knocked several ornaments off the Christmas tree with his tail. They raced out into the front hall, through the den and dining room, up and down the stairs twice, and then straight into the kitchen.

Mr. Callahan was standing at the counter, making himself a roast beef sandwich for lunch. "Hey!" he said, mildly, and pointed a table knife covered with low-fat mayonnaise at them. "No, no, no! That is very bad."

The dog stopped short. Bad? Mr. Callahan thought he was *bad*. He sank down to the floor, instantly very discouraged.

"She leads you into wicked ways, Santa Paws," Mr. Callahan told him. "It's really not good."

The dog's ears went up and he wagged his tail, when he heard the word "good." He *enjoyed* the word "good." It was one of his favorites.

Abigail leaped onto the kitchen table, where the other family cat, Evelyn, was already sitting. Evelyn hissed at her, and jumped over to the counter, instead.

"All right, all right," Mr. Callahan said. "Will you three be good, well-behaved animals, if I give you each a treat?"

The dog loved treats, and he was delighted to sit and accept a chunk of roast beef. Yay! It tasted great! Evelyn took her piece into the dining room, so that she could eat by herself. Abigail, who never liked to cooperate, used her front paw to push her tidbit lazily back and forth across the table. Then she pounced on it, growled softly, and batted it away again.

2

"She's an oddball, Santa Paws," Mr. Callahan said, as he recapped the mayonnaise jar and spread some lettuce leaves on top of two slices of homemade rye bread. "That's all I have to say."

The dog thumped his tail against the floor, alert for the possibility of more roast beef. He was tempted to steal Abigail's share of meat, but she would probably scratch him across the nose if he did. He watched her very carefully, though, in case she might drop it. Then, as far as he was concerned, it was his.

Mr. Callahan finished preparing his lunch by placing three dill pickles on his plate, along with his sandwich and some taco chips. He also poured himself a glass of skim milk, and then carried his tray out of the kitchen.

Santa Paws followed him into the living room and took a strategic position near the couch. He knew it would be rude to beg, but he still liked to be within easy range of food. *Any* food. Just in case.

Sharing lunch with Mr. Callahan was always fun. Of course, he enjoyed *everything* he did with the Callahans. They were the best family in the world! He had lived with them for almost three whole years. Wow!

When he was a puppy, he had been a stray on the streets of Oceanport. He hated being by himself, and he was always very hungry and cold.

Then, one lucky afternoon, he met a boy named Gregory Callahan on the elementary school playground. Gregory, and his big sister Patricia, brought him wonderful meaty cans of food to eat, and the dog ended up going to live at their house. Ever since then, he had always been happy. He *loved* Gregory and Patricia! He also loved Mr. and Mrs. Callahan — and Abigail and Evelyn. They all had lots of exciting adventures together.

Mr. Callahan was a writer, so he stayed home every day and worked on his new computer. He was still learning how to use it, and the dog hurried out of the room whenever he heard Mr. Callahan shout, "Oh, no! Come back!" at the disappearing file on his monitor screen. The dog liked it much better when Mr. Callahan spent hours lying on the couch, reading books or watching old movies on television. For some reason, this always seemed to make him very tired, and he and the dog would both take long naps.

Mrs. Callahan taught physics at Oceanport High School, which meant that she was gone during the day. She was very nice, and almost always remembered to feed him at exactly the same time every evening. The dog got very nervous if his supper was late for any reason. Mrs. Callahan also brushed his fur regularly with a set of fancy brushes, and she even made sure that his nails were never too long! Recently, she had bought him a brand-new royal blue collar and told him that he looked very handsome, indeed. "Handsome" was a happy word, and the dog wagged his tail enthusiastically whenever he heard it. "So, we have a blue-collar dog now," was Mr. Callahan's only comment.

Gregory was thirteen years old, and in the eighth grade this year. He was tall for his age, and very good at sports. Both he and Patricia had brown hair and blue eyes, just like their parents. Patricia was a year older than he was, and Mr. Callahan often said that she was "fourteen going on thirty." "Make that *forty*," Mrs. Callahan would say. Patricia's only response to this would be to lower her sunglasses — she almost *always* wore sunglasses, even indoors — for a second or two and look at them with benevolent pity.

Evelyn, who was a plump grey tiger cat, had lived with the Callahans even longer than he had! The dog was *pretty* sure that she loved him. Most of the time, anyway. Abigail was the newest member of the household. She was all black, with yellowish-orange eyes. When the dog had been lost the year before — mean, bad people *stole* him on purpose! — he had come across a tiny, abandoned kitten during his long journey home. He wasn't sure that he wanted a traveling companion — but she didn't leave him much choice in the matter. In fact, she gave him no choice whatsoever.

"Would you like a bite, Pumpkin?" Mr. Callahan asked suddenly, holding out part of his sandwich.

Mr. Callahan was the only one in the family who ever referred to him as Pumpkin. The dog wagged his tail and happily gulped the sandwich section down. He didn't like lettuce very much, but the rest of it was delicious. Even the mayonnaise.

Gregory had originally named him Nicholas, and everyone in the family had at least one special, private nickname for him. But mainly, they just called him "Santa Paws." All of the people in Oceanport seemed to know who he was, and they would always wave and shout "Hi, Santa Paws!" whenever they saw him in town. It was great to have so many friends!

After lunch and another long nap, the dog went out to the backyard for a run. It was snowing, and he had fun skidding through the one or two inches that had already fallen. But his paws got very cold, so he barked at the backdoor until Mr. Callahan came and let him into the house. The dog ate a Milk-Bone, drank some water from his red dish, and then crawled underneath Mr. Callahan's desk for a rest.

As the afternoon wore on, something terrible

happened. Mr. Callahan *left the house.* Alone! The dog had followed him out to the kitchen, waiting to hear the magic words, "Want to go for a ride in the car?" He wagged his tail tentatively, and held one front paw up in anticipation.

"You be a good dog, Santa Paws," Mr. Callahan said, as he put on a green plaid wool coat and a Bruins scarf. "Stay and guard the house."

Stay? The dog's tail dropped and he slowly sagged down to the floor. He had to stay home? By himself? This was awful!

Mr. Callahan smiled and bent down to pat him on the head. "It's okay, we'll all be back soon. Don't let Abigail break too many things."

Was *Abigail* going to get to go in the car instead of him? Oh, this was terrible. And unfair!

Mr. Callahan opened the door, glanced down at his feet, and sighed. He was still wearing his Tasmanian Devil slippers. He changed into his boots, gave Santa Paws another Milk-Bone, and then went outside.

The dog was so unhappy that he completely ignored his Milk-Bone. He kept his gaze on the door, hoping that Mr. Callahan would change his mind and come back. Abigail wandered over and gave one of his ears a light swat. The dog wasn't allowed to growl at cats — ever; for any reason — but he lifted his lip enough to show her one tooth. Abigail ignored this and kept whacking his ear.

7

The dog waited and waited and waited. And waited. The kitchen floor wasn't very comfortable, but he was determined to stay where he was until his family came home. It was his duty! He did eat his Milk-Bone, though.

After a while, Abigail got bored. She headed upstairs to take turns lying on everyone's pillows, although she stopped along the way to knock three round shiny ornaments off the Christmas tree, and to dash up and down the piano keyboard a couple of times. Evelyn just stayed on the loveseat in the den, sleeping.

The dog did his best to maintain his vigil, but he kept dozing off. When he heard the family station wagon — the Callahans thought SUVs were extremely silly, especially in the suburbs — and Mr. Callahan's old Buick sedan pulling into the driveway, he started barking joyfully. They were home! Yay!

Upstairs, there was a distinct thud as Abigail jumped off some bed or other, on her way downstairs. Evelyn would also probably join them, but the dog knew that she would take her time doing so.

The backdoor opened and Gregory came in, his hair and jacket covered with snow.

"Hey, boy!" he said. "You have a good day, pal?"

Good. Yes! The dog lifted his front paws so that he and Gregory could do their usual ritual of dancing around the kitchen together. Santa Paws was mostly German shepherd and weighed almost ninety pounds, so if he wasn't careful about jumping gently, he sometimes knocked people over by accident. Luckily, whenever it happened to Gregory, he just thought it was funny.

"Well, okay," Mrs. Callahan was saying to Patricia, as they entered the kitchen. "But I can't help thinking that maybe it would be better if you took it a little easier out there. It's only a game."

Patricia shrugged as she carried her hockey sticks and the heavy equipment bag over to the corner where the family stored their sports gear. "It's not my fault girls' hockey has so many dumb rules about body-checking. That's why I like playing co-ed better." In addition to being on the junior high girls team, this season Patricia had also joined a local Bantam hockey league.

"I know," Mrs. Callahan said, setting her brief-case and Patricia's book-crammed knapsack on the table. "It was just a little embarrassing to be sitting next to Mrs. Lewis when you plowed right through poor Harriet."

"She's much bigger than I am," Patricia said defensively. "And I didn't do it on purpose — I was just going for the puck."

Gregory laughed. "Yeah. Sure."

Patricia put her hands on her hips and turned

to glare at him. "I have just two words for you, Gregory. Hat. Trick."

"I have two words for *you*," Gregory said. "Penalty. Box."

"I really hope you two aren't fighting," Mr. Callahan said, as he lugged in an armload of snowy logs from the woodpile.

Gregory and Patricia liked to argue almost constantly, and it really got on their parents' nerves.

"Who, us?" Gregory asked. "No way."

"Never happen," Patricia agreed.

"Well, good," Mr. Callahan said. "Not exactly the holiday spirit." The wind was so strong outside that he closed the door with an effort. "It's really starting to come down out there."

Gregory looked worried and stopped dancing with Santa Paws for a minute. "Hey, whoa, what if they cancel school?"

"We'll spend the morning celebrating?" Patricia guessed.

"Yeah, but we have a game with Eastman on Friday," Gregory said. "I don't want to miss it." He was a starting forward on the Oceanport Junior High basketball team, and even though he wasn't as competitive as Patricia was, he still liked to play.

"It's two days away, Greg," Mrs. Callahan said. "Don't worry about it now."

There was a small television on the counter,

and she flipped it on to the Weather Channel. A gleeful reporter talked about the current snowstorm sweeping across southern New England, and promised unusually cold temperatures for the next week or so. He also pointed at a swirling cloud formation down near the Carolinas and predicted that New England might well be battered by a winter nor'easter once the storm had made its way up the coast. "Bundle up, folks! It could be quite a blustery Christmas!" he proclaimed with great enthusiasm.

Mrs. Callahan glanced at her husband. "Maybe you'd better bring some more wood in tonight, just in case."

"Oh, come on, Mom," Patricia said. "They *always* predict terrible storms, and then get all disappointed when they head out to sea, instead."

"Well, it can't hurt to be prepared," Mr. Callahan said, and put his coat back on. "Why don't you two come out and give me a hand?"

On their way outside, Gregory grabbed an old canvas tote bag from the row of hooks where they always hung their coats. Santa Paws liked being able to help, and by carrying the bag's handles, he could manage at least two small logs.

There were three or four inches of snow on the ground now, and more was falling steadily. The dog was so happy that his family was home, that he galloped around in circles.

While Mr. Callahan lifted the tarpaulin covering the woodpile, Gregory and Patricia started to gather kindling. Seeing the sticks, the dog got very excited — were they planning a game of fetch? He pranced over and grabbed one of the sticks, shaking it back and forth.

"Okay, pal," Gregory said, and threw it across the yard for him.

"I wish we could teach him to *collect* the sticks for us," Patricia said.

Their father looked up from the stack he was piling together for them to carry inside. "And chop and split the logs, while he's at it."

Gregory shook his head. "No way. Dogs should just have fun."

Santa Paws chased the stick down in the snow and ran back towards Gregory. Then suddenly, he stopped short, and let the stick drop out of his mouth. He listened and sniffed intently, as the hair rose up slightly on his back.

Something — somewhere — was very wrong!

2

Santa Paws had no idea *why* he could always
sense when people were in trouble, but over
the years, he had learned to listen to his instincts. In Oceanport — and all over New England, for that matter — he had the reputation
for being a hero. He never exactly planned to
rescue anyone, but it just seemed to work out
that way.

Once he had located the source of this particular problem, he ran towards the gate and sailed
over it into the driveway. Then he raced down
the street at top speed.

"Hey, whoa," Gregory said uneasily. "Santa
Paws! Come back!"

Patricia sighed. "Here we go again."

They ran after him, with Mr. Callahan lagging
only a few steps behind. Inside the house, Mrs.
Callahan glanced through the kitchen window
just in time to see her entire family tearing down
the street in the middle of the snowstorm. She

13

shook her head, and went back to throwing together a hamburger casserole for supper.

Santa Paws headed directly towards the Robinsons' house. Every year, the Robinsons liked to decorate their roof with dozens of strands of Christmas tree lights. Tonight, Mr. Robinson had noticed that some of his lights seemed to have burned out. So, he had come outside to fix them. Unfortunately, his ladder had slipped in the snow and fallen out of reach. Now Mr. Robinson was dangling helplessly from his roof! He had been shouting for help, but no one inside his house could hear him over the noise of the wind.

Santa Paws stopped directly below him and began barking.

"Oh, thank goodness, Santa Paws," Mr. Robinson said weakly. He wasn't sure he could hang on much longer! "Please, go get help!"

Santa Paws ran over to the front door and jumped against it, barking the whole time. His front paw grazed the doorbell by accident, and it rang loudly. After a moment, Mrs. Robinson opened the door.

"What is it, Santa Paws?" she asked curiously.

Santa Paws barked, and dashed around the side of the house. Mrs. Robinson followed him, and got there just as Gregory, Patricia, and Mr. Callahan arrived.

"Hang on, George!" Mr. Callahan said. He

quickly grabbed the ladder and raised it against the side of the house.

Mr. Robinson grabbed the rungs gratefully and slowly eased himself down to the snowy ground.

"Whew," he said, letting out his breath. "That was close." He smiled at the Callahans. "You really have a mighty fine dog there."

Gregory and Patricia were very pleased to hear the compliment, since *they* thought Santa Paws was the best dog in the world.

Mrs. Robinson looked quite annoyed. "George, I thought you were upstairs. Did you really have to come out here in the middle of the storm?"

"The lights were broken," Mr. Robinson said meekly.

Gregory noticed that the extension cord was dangling free, and showed it to Patricia. She shrugged and then plugged the cord back in. Instantly, all of the strands lit up with a bright, festive glow.

Mr. Robinson's face flushed. "Gosh, I think I'm just going to head on in for some supper now." He reached out to give Santa Paws a quick pat. "Good dog."

Santa Paws barked enthusiastically. Mr. Robinson was one of his friends!

"Thanks again, everyone," Mrs. Robinson said.

After exchanging goodnights, the Callahans walked back up the street, with Santa Paws in the lead.

"That was smart, Santa Paws," Gregory said proudly. "Way to go."

Santa Paws wagged his tail, because "smart" was yet another word that he liked very much.

When they carried their load of logs and kindling into the house a few minutes later, Mrs. Callahan looked up from the evening newspaper she was reading. Her casserole was already baking in the oven.

"Good rescue?" she asked.

"Average," Patricia said, as Gregory said, "*Excellent* rescue."

Mrs. Callahan looked at Mr. Callahan for confirmation one way or the other.

"George Robinson was about to fall off his house," he said.

Mrs. Callahan thought about that, nodded, and resumed reading the newspaper.

"Want a Milk-Bone, boy?" Gregory asked.

Santa Paws dropped his log-filled tote bag so that he could bark. Yes! A Milk-Bone would be just great!

What fun he was having!

After dinner, Gregory and Patricia had their nightly fight about whose turn it was to do the dishes and, as usual, Patricia won. She relented slightly, though, and agreed to dry the pans and set the table for breakfast.

When they were both finished, Patricia sat

down on the kitchen floor to clean and organize her hockey equipment. Since their favorite television program didn't come on for another twenty minutes, Gregory sat nearby to brush Santa Paws.

"Rachel thought it was really nice of you to keep crashing into the boards right near us today," he said.

Rachel was Patricia's best friend, and even though she was blind, she still always came to Patricia's games. "Well, she doesn't have a frame of reference for hockey," Patricia said, as she carefully wiped down her skate blades with a chamois cloth. "So I like to give her good sound effects."

Gregory laughed. "And make Mom and Dad nervous."

Patricia grinned sheepishly. "Maybe a little, yeah." She began unwinding the frayed black tape on her stick so that she could replace it with a fresh layer. "Rachel says you give really good color commentary."

"Hey, yo! A career!" Gregory said cheerfully.

"What happened to being a veterinarian?" Patricia asked.

"That'll be my *day* job," Gregory explained. He liked science — and animals — so he had always figured that being a vet was the way to go. As far as he knew, Patricia was still deciding among being an FBI agent, a Supreme Court

Justice — or a Vampire Slayer. Preferably a *rogue* slayer, of course.

When Patricia dropped the ball of old tape on the floor, Santa Paws promptly picked it up and gave Gregory a pleading look. He liked fetching *much better* than he liked being brushed.

"Okay," Gregory said, and threw the tape-ball down towards the pantry.

Santa Paws tore off to retrieve it, his paws skidding on the linoleum.

"How do you think he knows all the stuff he knows?" Gregory asked.

Patricia lifted an eyebrow. "What, you mean, *fetching*? Or the stock tips he gives me?" For her most recent birthday, their grandparents had opened a small online trading account for her — with the strict rule that she do absolutely *no* margin trading, under any circumstances. Patricia assured them that this would be no problem for her whatsoever, because she was purely "buy-and-hold" by nature. For some reason, her grandparents had found that hilarious.

Gregory shook his head and tossed the tape-ball again. "You know I mean the rescue stuff. How does he know?"

"Magic?" Patricia guessed.

That was actually Gregory's theory, but he would have felt dumb saying it aloud. "Well, it's pretty cool," he said.

Patricia nodded. "Yeah, it's definitely cool."

Mrs. Callahan came out to the kitchen, presumably to check on their cleaning efforts. She stepped smoothly to one side as Santa Paws careened past her on his way after the tape-ball again.

"Do you think Santa Paws is magic, Mom?" Gregory asked.

Mrs. Callahan edged further towards the wall as Santa Paws narrowly avoided her on his way back. "Actually, I think he's a little on the clumsy side, Greg," she said, with a smile.

"Okay," Gregory said, "but none of the *other* dogs in town do, you know, hero stuff."

"That's true," Mrs. Callahan conceded. "But I kind of hope he takes Christmas *off* this year, don't you? Wouldn't it be nice to have a quiet holiday for once?"

Gregory and Patricia nodded. It had been several *years* since they had had anything resembling a quiet holiday. Somehow, Santa Paws always seemed to be involved in unusually difficult adventures every Christmas. With luck, this year would be different.

They *hoped*.

By the next morning, the snow had stopped, leaving a picturesque six inches on the ground. A traditional holiday singing performance was going to be held on the village green that night, and the Callahans were planning to attend. The town of Oceanport was very conscious of its diverse population and multi-cultural background. During the month of December, there was always a special exhibit in the park called "The Festival of Many Lands." That way, everyone's heritage could be celebrated, instead of simply focusing on Christmas. Oceanport took the notion of America's being a melting pot *very* much to heart.

When Gregory and Patricia got home from their respective team practices, they heard a familiar — and dreaded — sound as they walked into the kitchen. Off in the den, their father was playing Frank Sinatra. He *always* played Frank Sinatra when he was working. Seven days a week, fifty-two weeks a year, rain or snow or shine — the house was filled with the sounds of Frank, Frank, *Frank*.

Mrs. Callahan was sitting at the kitchen table, correcting papers to hand back before the holiday vacation. Once they had told her about how their days had gone, and spent a few minutes patting Santa Paws, Gregory gestured towards the den.

"I guess, um, Dad's working, right?" he asked.

"Either that, or singing to himself," Mrs. Callahan said.

Gregory and Patricia nodded grimly. Mr. Callahan did a lot of singing to himself. It was usually a sign that he had writer's block and was in a very foul mood.

"You know, Frank did Christmas songs," Patricia said. "Couldn't he at least play Frank's Christmas CDs?"

"You would think," Mrs. Callahan agreed, concentrating on her papers.

Gregory and Patricia decided to take this as a no. Besides, they had snacks to eat, television to watch, and email to check. On top of which, over the years — no matter how much they complained — they had actually grown rather fond of Frank.

For a special treat, Mrs. Callahan ordered take-out from one of their favorite restaurants, Nuestra Casa del Taco. After dinner, they were going to meet their Aunt Emily and her three-year-old daughter, Miranda, at the municipal park. Their Uncle Steve was on duty tonight with the Oceanport Police Department, but he was in charge of crowd control at the concert, so they would see him, too. Uncle Steve was Mr. Callahan's little brother.

Since the celebration was being held outdoors, Santa Paws could come, too. He leaped into the backseat of the car with great excitement, wondering what sort of adventure was ahead of them. They *always* went someplace interesting and fun!

"Dad, you're going to have to listen to *ordinary* singers," Patricia said, as Mr. Callahan parked the station wagon on Main Street. "Think you can handle it?"

"Brought my Walkman, just in case," he said cheerfully.

Mrs. Callahan stared at him. "Tell me you didn't."

Instead of answering, Mr. Callahan just grinned.

It was very cold, but the sky was perfectly clear and filled with stars. Holiday lights reflected off the fresh snow, and as they walked towards the park, they could already hear the Oceanport Amateur Brass Band tuning up. The band would be accompanying the Village Adult Choir — whose star soloist was a nine-year-old boy named James.

Lots of people said hello to the Callahans, but *everyone* they passed had an enthusiastic greeting for Santa Paws. The dog happily wagged his tail, shook paws with anyone who asked, and posed for pictures with small children.

Gregory watched him, shaking his head. "He could run for Mayor," he said to Patricia. "He could *win*."

"Sure," Patricia agreed. "As long as he held down property taxes."

Gregory wasn't quite sure what that meant, but his parents seemed to find it very funny.

The park was so crowded that they had a hard time making their way over to the Bodhi Day Buddhist exhibit, where they had planned to meet Aunt Emily and Miranda. But first, they ran into Uncle Steve, who was giving several other local police officers their sector assignments. Right now, he was a Sergeant, but he was hoping to move up to Lieutenant after the next promotional exam.

"Traffic control is going to be our main issue," he was saying, "but — "

"Hi, Uncle Steve!" Gregory yelled in his direction.

Uncle Steve looked over and waved. He had the same dark, thick hair Mr. Callahan had, but he was much more muscular and didn't wear glasses. "Hey, everyone," he said, and nodded towards Santa Paws. "Glad to see you brought the canine ESU. You never know when we might need him." ESU stood for "Emergency Services Unit."

Mr. Callahan shook his head quickly. "No, he's taking the holidays off this year."

"Very much so," Mrs. Callahan agreed.

"Well, I'd say he's certainly earned the vacation time," Uncle Steve answered. Two years earlier, Santa Paws had saved *his* life — along with Gregory and Patricia — after their private plane crashed, and that was something that Uncle Steve would never forget. "Emily took Miranda over to look at the Father Christmas in Lapland exhibit, but she said she'd be right back."

"As you were, then," Patricia said, to the great amusement of all of the police officers.

Uncle Steve gave her a salute. "Yes, ma'am."

Patricia grinned and saluted back. She had always thought that she just might end up being a police officer someday — except that she wanted to get her PhD, first. "Carry on."

While Uncle Steve continued briefing the officers, the Callahans headed for the Buddhist exhibit. It had been sponsored by the Oceanport Zen Center, and honored the Buddha's Day of Enlightenment. The Festival of Many Lands included every form of holiday celebration imaginable. The exhibit next to the Buddhist one was about the Frost King legend in Scandinavia, and displays honoring Kwanzaa and Germany's St. Thomas Day were right across from them. Gregory went to look at the Kwanzaa exhibit, because that was the holiday his best friend Oscar celebrated. In fact, Oscar's mother was a graphics artist, and she had been the head designer of the booth this year. As far as Gregory could tell, she had done a really good job.

Miranda came toddling over, wearing a bright red wool coat and eating a candy cane. Aunt Emily, looking very weary, was hurrying after her. Aunt Emily worked full-time at an advertising agency in Boston, and since she was seven months pregnant, she was feeling pretty harried lately.

"Merry Christmas!" Miranda said. "We saw reindeer!"

"You did? Wow," Mr. Callahan said, and swung her up into his arms. "Can you show them to me, buttercup?" Then he carried her back towards the Lapland exhibit, which had been designed by Oceanport's Finnish-American Society.

Aunt Emily sat down gratefully on a nearby bench to rest. "She *never* gets tired," she remarked to Mrs. Callahan.

Mrs. Callahan smiled wryly, and glanced at Gregory and Patricia. "And they *never* grow out of it."

Gregory and Patricia did their best to look innocent — and remarkably well-behaved. Then Patricia noticed her friend Rachel standing near the *Feliz Navidad* display with her mother.

"Rachel, over here!" she called. "Your eight o'clock." Because Rachel was blind, she could get around much more easily if she used the concept of a clock to help herself navigate.

Rachel started towards them, using her cane. She had desperately wanted a guide dog for years, but none of the training schools would let her attend until she turned sixteen. Since she had expected to be allowed to go when she turned *twelve*, the idea of waiting so much longer had been terribly disappointing to her. Like Patricia, she was only fourteen now, so she still had two years to go. But she always moved quite gracefully on her cane, and lots of times, people never even noticed that she couldn't see.

Since it was so crowded, Patricia moved out to meet her halfway.

"Do you think this concert is going to be even *remotely* cool?" Rachel asked.

"No," Patricia said instantly. "But we can stand around and be, you know, quietly sarcastic and all."

Rachel nodded. "Okay, good. We can make fun of Greg, too, if we get bored."

"Hey!" Gregory protested. "I heard that!"

But before the conversation could escalate into a quarrel, the choir began to file up onto the bandstand. Seeing this, the entire crowd quieted down instantly. Just as the choir burst into a rousing version of "Hark the Herald Angels Sing," Mr. Callahan brought Miranda back over to join the rest of the family.

The dog sat next to Gregory, leaning heavily against his leg. Gregory reached down and rested a gloved hand on top of his head. The dog always liked that, especially when Gregory rubbed his ears gently. It was also nice to be outside, surrounded by so many smiling people. The music was making him feel sleepy, so he yawned widely and decided to take a nap.

"You can't look bored at town functions, Santa Paws," Patricia said. "You just blew the election."

Santa Paws wagged his tail at her, and then closed his eyes again. He was having a really happy dream about being given *three* whole dishes of food for supper, when his eyes suddenly flew back open.

There was trouble in the air!

3

The dog jumped to his feet and cocked his head to concentrate on all of the different scents nearby and decide which one was bothering him. There were *so* many people around. It was confusing! Then he let out one sharp bark, and began running towards Main Street.

"Oh, no," Gregory groaned, and his parents both sighed deeply.

"What is it?" Rachel asked, hearing the commotion.

"Santa Paws just took off," Patricia said. "Something must be going on."

Surprisingly, almost no one nearby noticed any of this, although a couple of people cheerfully said, "Bye, Santa Paws!" as he dashed away. Gregory was trying to follow him, but he was making much slower progress through the crowd. Since Mr. Callahan was still holding Miranda, Mrs. Callahan went after them this time.

Police Officers Lee and Bronkowski were stationed near the park entrance. When Santa Paws tore past them, they exchanged glances.

"That's not good," Officer Lee said thoughtfully.

"Not good at all," Officer Bronkowski agreed, and she reached for her radio to report this alarming development.

Santa Paws headed directly for Main Street. He wormed his way around parked cars and scrambled through thick drifts of plowed snow. There were bad people on the loose, and he had to stop them! He really didn't *like* bad people, especially after the horrible time when he had been stolen.

Just up Main Street, there were three boys from the high school who were trying to break into the parked cars. They were taking advantage of everyone being at the concert to steal CD players and radios, plus any Christmas presents they could find. Lots of people had gone Christmas shopping on Main Street before the concert, and left the bags in their cars. The boys didn't *need* any of these things — they just thought it would be fun to take them. Oceanport was such a quiet little town that many people regularly forgot to lock their cars, even though they should probably know better. On the other hand, the three boys — Michael Smith and his friends

Luke and Rich Crandall — also enjoyed breaking windows, so they didn't even *care* if the cars were locked.

Michael was flipping through a stack of CDs on the front seat of a Volvo, while Luke tried to get into the Jeep Cherokee behind it. Rich was shaking up a can of red spray paint, so that he could vandalize a Toyota. The Callahans' car was parked only two cars away!

Santa Paws loped up behind the boys and let out a low growl. He *knew* these boys, because he had had to chase them away from the Nativity scene in the park a long time ago, when he was a lost puppy.

Michael turned to see who was growling at them, and then sighed. "Look out, guys. It's that stupid Santa Paws."

Rich pointed the spray can at him. "*Bad dog!* Go home!"

Bad? He was *not* bad. The dog growled and took a menacing step closer.

"You know what? I really don't like this dog," Luke said. "There's no way to have fun in this town with him around." Luke had been using a crowbar to try to pry car trunks open, and he raised it to swing at Santa Paws.

Just then, Gregory finally caught up to Santa Paws.

"Hey!" he said, out of breath. "Leave my dog alone!"

"Who's going to make us?" Rich asked with a sneer.

Even though the boys were a lot bigger than he was, Gregory wasn't afraid. But he *did* kind of wish Patricia had come along, since she was really good at acting fierce. He, personally, hadn't had much practice. "*I* am," he said, clenching his fists tentatively.

Luke laughed. "Oh, yeah?" He swung the crowbar in the dog's direction, and Santa Paws dodged out of the way. "You, and what army?"

Santa Paws growled deep in his throat and moved to stand protectively in front of Gregory. Luke and Rich looked at each other uncertainly, and then retreated a couple of steps.

"Come on," Michael said, trying to encourage them. "We really going to let some *kid* and a dumb dog scare us off?"

"Well, boys, as it happens, *I'm* part of their army," a very calm voice said.

They all turned to see Mrs. Callahan standing a few steps away, with her arms folded across her chest. She was clearly *not* amused by the situation.

"Um, we were just kidding, Mrs. Callahan," Luke mumbled. He dropped his crowbar and tried to kick it underneath a car, out of sight.

Seeing this, Rich quickly shoved his spray can into a snowbank. All three boys knew Mrs. Callahan from the high school — and knew her quite well, since they had each stayed back a year.

"Yeah, we, uh, we like dogs," Michael said.

"And kids," Luke added. "We like kids."

"We *love* kids," Rich said. "*All* kids."

Uncle Steve and two other officers arrived now on foot, while Officers Lee and Bronkowski pulled up in their squad car. Mrs. Callahan frowned at Uncle Steve and looked pointedly at her watch.

"I know, it wasn't the world's greatest response time," he said sheepishly. "We had a little communications problem." Then he grinned at her. "I have to say, though — I had no idea you could run that fast."

"Yeah, really," one of the other officers chimed in, as he struggled to catch his breath. "She's got *wheels.*"

"Yes, well, I was in a hurry," Mrs. Callahan said, and looked a little self-conscious. "Is it all right if we go back to the concert now?"

Uncle Steve nodded, as Officer Lee ushered the three boys into the backseat of the squad car. "Sure thing — we'll take it from here."

"So, wait, I'm like, an eye-witness," Gregory said uncomfortably. "Am I going to have to testify?"

Uncle Steve grinned again. "Don't worry about it. I think we'll start off by calling their parents down to the station for a nice, long talk."

"I'm willing to testify," Gregory assured him. "For, you know, civic responsibility."

Uncle Steve looked at Mrs. Callahan. "Exactly how much television do you let them watch?"

Mrs. Callahan chose to ignore that. "Come on, Greg, come on, Santa Paws. Let's go back to the park."

The dog wagged his tail. Were they going for a walk now? Yay!

A few minutes later, they rejoined the rest of the family.

"Heroism run amuck?" Mr. Callahan asked his wife quietly.

"More or less," she said. "Be nice if he *could* take a little vacation."

Overhearing that, Patricia nudged Gregory. "So, should they — " she indicated the choir — "start singing, 'He knows when you've been bad or good, so be good for goodness sake?' "

"*Definitely*," Gregory said, and patted Santa Paws fondly.

Instead, the choir began a lively rendition of "I Have a Little Dreidel." Santa Paws turned around three times, settled comfortably against Gregory's leg, and closed his eyes.

After all of the excitement, he *really* needed another nap.

The concert concluded without further incident — much to the Callahans' relief. By the time they got home, everyone was hungry. So they had a late night snack of grilled cheese sandwiches, hot chocolate, Milk-Bones for Santa Paws, and some tuna fish for the cats. After that, since they were really tired and tomorrow was the last day of school before winter vacation, Gregory and Patricia headed upstairs to go to sleep. Santa Paws had already conked out, sprawling across the crocheted quilt on Gregory's bed.

"So many rescues, so little time," Patricia said.

Gregory nodded. No *wonder* Santa Paws rested almost constantly. Then again, the cats also slept about eighteen hours a day — and had very little excuse. Then he shook his head. "Boy, you should have seen her — Mom was going to *pound* those guys."

Patricia laughed, doing her best to imagine the scene. "Well, you'd better believe I'm going to remind her next time she yells at me for being too rough at hockey."

"The next time I foul out, too," Gregory said. Although he usually fouled out due to *clumsiness*, not because he was aggressive. Whenever he fell over his own feet, his father said not to worry about it, that he was just growing too fast right now — and the same thing had happened to him when he was thirteen. Then again, his father was *still* a klutz, which Gregory figured might not bode too well for his own future.

"See you tomorrow," Patricia said, as she went into her room.

"You need protecting in the middle of the night, you just call me," Gregory advised.

"I think I'll call *Mom*," Patricia said.

They both laughed, and headed off to bed.

The next morning, the temperature was near the freezing level, and the sky was covered with thick, grey clouds. Both Gregory and Patricia had overslept, so breakfast was very hectic. Today was the last day of school before vacation, and the next day was Christmas Eve! Mrs. Callahan was trying to get everyone organized, while Mr. Callahan talked on the telephone to his early-rising editor in New York.

"No, I really don't want to change that sentence," he said, and then listened briefly. "Well, because it's crucial. Losing it would destroy the entire narrative drive of the book." Then he listened some more. "Oh, no, I don't think so. I like *that* sentence, too, frankly."

Gregory shook his head, as he grabbed a Pop-Tart to eat in the car. "Writers, man. *Way* too uptight."

Mrs. Callahan was waiting impatiently by the door, because she didn't want to be late. "Do you have your history homework?" she asked him.

"No, I forgot," he said, and turned to go back upstairs.

"What about your uniform?" she asked when he returned.

Gregory winced. "Right. Okay." He went upstairs again.

"And get a sweater!" Mrs. Callahan called after him. "You might need it later." She looked at Patricia, who was finding this whole exchange pretty funny. "Algebra assignment?"

Patricia nodded.

"Lunch money?" Mrs. Callahan asked.

Patricia nodded.

"Book report?" Mrs. Callahan asked.

Patricia started to nod, then blushed slightly and rushed upstairs. Mrs. Callahan sighed and leaned against the backdoor to wait for them.

"*That* sentence, too?" Mr. Callahan was saying. "I don't understand. Don't you like *any* of them?"

Once Gregory and Patricia were back in the kitchen, they all said good-bye to Mr. Callahan, who smiled and gave them a distracted wave. Then, Mrs. Callahan opened the door and ushered Gregory and Patricia outside.

"Car keys?" Patricia asked, once they were all in the driveway.

Mrs. Callahan grinned wryly. "Right," she said, and went back to get them.

So far, they were all having a rather stressful day.

* * *

Throughout the morning, the winds picked up, until the windows of the house began to rattle. Santa Paws and the cats were getting increasingly edgy, and they all kept pacing nervously from room to room. Sometimes thunderstorms frightened them, and this winter storm seemed to be having the same effect so far.

Mr. Callahan was trying to work, and this endless animal activity was distracting him.

"Come on, lie down," he kept telling them. "Good dog. Good cats. Please lie down."

They would obey for a few minutes — and then start prowling around again. By midafternoon, a hard, sleety snow had begun falling. Ice was clattering against the windows, and Santa Paws whined softly.

"It's just a storm," Mr. Callahan said reassuringly. "Nothing to worry about. Who wants a snack?"

A gust of frigid wind came rushing down the chimney, and Evelyn streaked upstairs in dismay. She hid deep inside the linen closet and curled into a tight ball to try and sleep. Abigail examined the dish of chicken catfood Mr. Callahan fixed for her, but then ignored it. Santa Paws accepted a Milk-Bone politely, but he just carried the treat around, instead of lying down to eat it the way he normally would. All of this was starting to unnerve Mr. Callahan a little, and he decided that he wasn't hungry, either.

The lights flickered every so often, indicating that the power was probably going to go out soon. Mr. Callahan quickly saved everything to disk, and shut his computer down. He wasn't going to take any chances of losing his latest revisions! Then he turned on the television to see delighted weather announcers discussing "the real corker of a nor'easter currently slamming into the New England coast." They were predicting a small accumulation of snow, lots of ice, and very dangerous road conditions. For the time being, there was a Winter Storm Advisory being issued.

"Maybe you should go out now," Mr. Callahan said to Santa Paws. "Before it gets any worse."

The dog shrank down on his rug, as though he were trying to make himself invisible. He didn't like storms — *any* storms. He especially didn't like *this* storm.

"Come on, Pumpkin," Mr. Callahan said heartily. "I'll go with you and bring in some more wood."

The dog slowly dragged himself to his feet and slogged reluctantly after him. When Mr. Callahan pulled the door open, more cold wind blew into the house. The dog shivered and retreated back towards the den.

"Okay," Mr. Callahan said. "I'm not going to make you, Santa Paws."

There were already lots of branches strewn

around the yard, and the footing was very slippery. Mr. Callahan walked carefully as he carried several loads of wood inside. He put the logs in the back hall, where they could dry off without dripping water all over the house.

The dog bravely joined Mr. Callahan on his fourth trip out to the wood pile. But just as he stepped outside, a huge branch snapped off a nearby tree and came crashing to the ground about ten feet away from him. The dog yelped and ran to huddle against the backdoor.

This storm was scary!

4

Mr. Callahan gathered up one final armload of logs and brought them, along with Santa Paws, into the house. He forced the backdoor shut, fighting against the powerful winds, and then locked it.

"I really hope we don't lose any trees out there," he said, looking concerned. There had been a pretty strong hurricane a few months earlier, and many of the trees in the yard — and all over Oceanport — had been badly damaged. It would not take very much wind to knock some of them over. He reached down to pat Santa Paws on the head. "Anyway. How about a Milk-Bone, boy?"

The dog took the bone without much enthusiasm and slunk into the den to lie underneath Mr. Callahan's desk. Abigail, who was also feeling jittery, crawled in next to him. The lights flickered again, but then came back on. Every instinct the dog had told him that this was a *terrible* storm

— and he wanted it to be over. Until then, he just felt like hiding.

People who lived in New England were accustomed to ferocious storms. In fact, most of them *liked* bad weather. Mr. Callahan — along with his wife and children — was no exception to this. Whenever there was a huge storm in Oceanport, the first thing everyone liked to do was run down to the seawall to see how big the waves were. But he still couldn't help wondering why Santa Paws and the cats seemed so unnerved. After all, animals were usually very good at sensing things that human beings didn't even notice. Could this storm be worse than the typical winter nor'easter?

First, he tried calling the junior high school to see if classes were going to be dismissed early. The number was busy, so other parents were probably doing the same thing. He watched a few more weather reports, ate a blueberry muffin, and unloaded the dishwasher. The sleet still seemed pretty heavy, but not particularly alarming. Finally, for lack of a better idea, he put a call in to the Oceanport Police Department and asked to speak to Sergeant Callahan.

"What's up?" his little brother asked cheerfully, when he came on the line.

"Have you heard anything about this storm?" Mr. Callahan asked.

"Not really," Steve said. "The last report we

got said that it was probably going to blow out to sea."

"Hmmm." Mr. Callahan frowned. "The last report *I* heard said that it was going to intensify."

"Well, we'll probably have a few fender-benders," Steve said. "So we'll be out there on the roads making sure people slow down tonight."

Mr. Callahan kept frowning as he looked at Santa Paws hunched underneath his desk. "Okay. I was just — okay."

"Since when does a little sleet make you nervous?" Steve wanted to know.

"It's not *me*," Mr. Callahan said, somewhat defensively. "But — well, the animals have been acting very strange today."

"Your pets are all *extremely* strange animals," Steve pointed out.

"Well, yeah," Mr. Callahan conceded. After all, it was hard to argue with that. "But I don't think I've ever seen Santa Paws this tense."

"It's probably just the wind that's bothering him," Steve said. "I think it affects their ears."

Mr. Callahan wasn't quite so sure about that, but after talking for a while about their various Christmas plans, he hung up. Then he went over and crouched down next to his desk. He hadn't realized that Abigail was hiding there, too, and he patted both of them.

"Take it easy, okay?" he said. "There's no reason to be scared. Everything's going to be fine."

Then he sat back down in front of the television to keep an eye on the latest weather reports. Santa Paws and Abigail climbed up next to him, and Abigail tucked her head underneath his elbow. Mr. Callahan frowned again. Granted, they might not be the world's most ordinary animals, but this was *still* very peculiar behavior.

Santa Paws snuggled very close to Mr. Callahan. The dog was very glad to be indoors, where it was *safe*. He just hoped that this storm would be over soon.

Over at the junior high school, school had just ended for the day. Gregory had been afraid that his basketball game would be canceled because of the weather, but so far, they were still scheduled to leave on the team bus promptly at three o'clock. Home games were more fun, because then his family always came to cheer him on. It was kind of interesting to play in other gymnasiums, though. Somehow, even though the courts were regulation size, each one felt very different, and changed the energy of the game.

Gregory and his best friend, Oscar, went straight to their lockers to get their coats and their gym bags. They would change into their uniforms at their opponent's school. They were playing the Eastman Junior High School Sharks — a team that was both better, and *taller*, than the Oceanport Mariners were.

"We're going to lose today, Greg," Oscar said glumly. Oscar played point guard on the team, and he and Gregory had been best friends since kindergarten. They both liked basketball, but they spent much more time talking about football, which was their favorite sport. "We're going to lose *big*."

Gregory thought so, too, but he didn't want to admit it. "Well, Coach gave us all those new plays. Maybe we'll get lucky."

"Hey, I'm just hoping we don't get embarrassed," Oscar said, and paused. "Can you *remember* any of the new plays?"

"Um, not really," Gregory confessed. "I kind of get confused when he writes all that stuff with the Xs and the Os."

Oscar nodded. "Me, too. And I'm the one who's supposed to be reading the other team's defenses and all."

Gregory had to grin, since whenever he got nervous on the court, Oscar inevitably forgot everything he knew about basketball and started shouting out football terminology. When he would yell something like "nickel defense!" or "look out, flea-flicker!", *both* teams would usually stop what they were doing and look at the sidelines for an explanation.

44

Suddenly, his locker-door slammed shut right in front of his face. Gregory flinched, but it was only Patricia's way of saying hello.

"Just wanted to wish you children good luck at your game," she said, her voice very chipper.

Gregory opened his locker again and wedged the door open with his knee, so she couldn't slam it again. "Thanks, old lady. Are you going right home?" he asked. Her hockey practices weren't scheduled to resume again until after the holidays.

Patricia made a face. "No. I have to stay after and wash Mrs. O'Leary's blackboards, first."

"You volunteered for that?" Oscar asked, sounding skeptical.

"No, I guess you'd call it — a command performance," Patricia said.

"That a code word for 'detention'?" Gregory asked, checking to make sure he had everything he needed in his knapsack.

Patricia nodded wryly. "Yeah. She says she doesn't like my attitude. Or my handwriting." She paused. "Or my sunglasses."

"Go figure," Oscar said.

Patricia magnanimously decided to overlook that remark. "So I'm supposed to 'think it over,' while I clean up her classroom." She glanced at Gregory. "Don't tell Mom and Dad, okay?"

"They'd probably think she was a grinch for making you do it on the last day before vacation, anyway," Gregory said.

"Well, they'd be right." Patricia checked her watch. "Oh, great. Now I'm even late showing up."

Gregory leaned over so that he could see the time, too. "Whoa, so are we. Come on, Oscar, we don't want to miss the bus. Tell Dad I'll call from Eastman when we're on our way back here so he can pick me up, okay?"

"Okay," Patricia said. "Hope you guys have a good game."

As they ran off, she sighed and headed towards the eighth grade wing. Because she was late, Mrs. O'Leary was probably going to make her wash all of the *desks*, too.

At the high school, Mrs. Callahan had to attend a mandatory teachers' meeting before she would be able to go home for the day. Then she was going to stop at the mall and pick up some last-minute Christmas presents. Every year, she planned to get all of her shopping done early — and every single year, she ended up still having presents left to buy on Christmas Eve.

When she called home to check in, she wasn't at all surprised to hear that the animals were behaving oddly, but the fact that there was a major storm going on *did* come as news. The high school building was only one story high, and had been designed with very few windows. Anyone who was inside could go all day without getting anywhere near a window. This atmosphere was supposed to promote good concentration, but mainly, it just caused claustrophobia.

"Are Gregory and Patricia home yet?" she asked.

"No, but I'm expecting them any minute," Mr. Callahan answered. "I'm sure Gregory's game was postponed, but I'll call the school and make sure."

"Do you think they'll be okay walking home?" Mrs. Callahan asked.

"Sure," Mr. Callahan said. "It's not that bad yet. The dog has just been making me nervous, that's all."

Mrs. Callahan laughed. "Better the dog, than your manuscript."

"Well, now that you mention it . . ." Mr. Callahan said, letting his voice trail off sadly, and Mrs. Callahan laughed again.

Before they hung up, Mr. Callahan promised that he would get dinner started and warned her to drive extra-safely.

"Maybe you should pick up some milk and bread, too," he said.

That was an old Southern New England joke, since whenever there was even a *hint* of bad weather approaching, many people often rushed out immediately to stock up milk and bread. No one was exactly sure why those two specific items had been singled out for special attention over the years — but it happened without fail during every storm.

"I was thinking more along the lines of plenty of chips and Twinkies," Mrs. Callahan answered. "But I'll get a half gallon of skim, if that would make you happy."

"That would be peachy," Mr. Callahan said. He was very fond of chips.

Once she was off the phone, Mrs. Callahan automatically looked around the windowless teachers' room.

"Did you know that there's a terrible storm going on outside?" she asked Mr. Jarvis, one of the French teachers.

Mr. Jarvis also looked around at the painted cement block walls, and then shrugged. "If you say so."

Mrs. Callahan wanted to go check outside, but it was time for the teachers' meeting, which was being held in the — windowless — library. If anyone brought up new business at the meeting, maybe she would suggest that they try to find enough money in the budget to put in some *sky-lights*.

When Mr. Callahan finally got through to the main office at the junior high, he was very upset to hear that Gregory and the rest of the team had already left for their game. Eastman was about twenty miles away, and he didn't like the idea of Gregory being out on the road with such icy conditions. Actually, he would feel a lot better when the *whole family* was back home, safe and sound.

All of the television stations were now officially issuing Winter Storm Warnings and Traveler's Advisories. The latest radar indicated that the storm was gathering strength, because of a low-pressure system. High winds and sleet were predicted to continue for the rest of the afternoon and throughout the night. The coastal areas north of Boston — in other words, Oceanport and the other nearby towns — were expected to be especially hard hit by this nor'easter. People were being instructed to stay inside and wait for further updates.

It always got dark early during the winter, but the storm made it seem as though dusk had already fallen. A light sheen of ice was covering all of the trees in the backyard, and the patio also had a visible layer of ice on top of the shoveled snow.

As he peered out the kitchen window, Santa Paws came over and nudged Mr. Callahan's leg anxiously with his muzzle. He could tell that Mr. Callahan was troubled, and he wondered if they were *both* worrying about the storm.

"Good dog," Mr. Callahan said, almost as a reflex. "It's okay, everyone's going to be home soon."

The dog whimpered quietly in response. Where was Gregory? Where was Patricia? Why weren't they here yet? When would they come?

Mr. Callahan let out his breath. He was finding Santa Paws' distress extremely contagious. "Well, it's not going to help if we stand around here and stare out the window," he said aloud. "Come on, we'll go do something constructive."

There were plenty of storm preparations that he could make. The faucets should all be turned on slightly to prevent the pipes from freezing, the bathtubs and kitchen pans could be filled with fresh water, and it would also be a good idea to gather up as many spare candles and batteries as possible.

Besides, Mr. Callahan knew that the best strategy to keep from worrying was to stay busy!

Mrs. O'Leary had been very cross when Patricia arrived ten minutes late for detention. So she told Patricia to wash the blackboards and desks in the adjoining classrooms, too. With a very mature effort, Patricia managed not to ask her if she should scrub the floors with an old toothbrush while she was at it — or drop and give her twenty push-ups.

When she finally finished and had rinsed out the sponge and bucket, Mrs. O'Leary was waiting behind her desk and tapping her foot impatiently. She was young and blond and very fashionably dressed, but somehow, her rather cranky personality did not fit her chic appearance.

"*Well?*" she asked.

"I'm all finished, ma'am," Patricia said politely.

"I see." Mrs. O'Leary looked her over with a very critical gaze. "Am I going to have to speak to your parents again, Patricia, or are you going to come back to school with a better attitude?"

"I'm going to mend my ways, ma'am," Patricia said, with enough sweetness to hide any potential sarcasm. "I have a whole new outlook."

Mrs. O'Leary wasn't buying *that* for a second, but after a long pause, she nodded. "Very well," she said. "You may go home now. Do you have a ride?"

"Um, yeah," Patricia answered. "I'm all set, thank you." Actually, she was afraid that she would get in trouble if she called home and admitted she'd had detention, so she would just walk. It was only about a mile and a half to her house from the school.

Once Patricia got outside and saw the ice everywhere, she almost turned around and went back to call her father. But he might still be in a bad mood about his book revisions, and she didn't want to bother him. Naturally, she *also* didn't want him to yell at her. Besides, if she hurried, she might be able to get home before he even noticed how late she was. As a rule, he lost track of time when he was working.

So she pulled up her hood, zipped her Patriots jacket, and started walking. The ground was very slippery, and it occurred to her that maybe today hadn't been the best day to wear shiny-soled cowboy boots. Still, she only fell once during the first block and a half, and figured that was a pretty good average.

The sleet felt more like hail as it pounded down. Everything was covered with a glaze of ice, and it actually looked kind of pretty. The trees were iced right down to the smallest twigs, as though they had been sprayed with a fine covering of glass.

As headlights came down the street in her direction, Patricia instinctively moved away from the curb and closer to a nearby hedge. The car slowed as it approached, and Patricia saw that Mrs. O'Leary was behind the wheel. Unfortunately, when she stepped on the brakes, the car skidded on the ice. Mrs. O'Leary pressed harder on the brakes, and the car began to spin out of control.

For a perplexed second, Patricia just watched the car skid, and then she realized what was happening.

It was coming right towards her!

5

When Patricia saw that the car was hurtling right over the curb, she tried to jump over the thick hedge out of harm's way. She managed to get partway over, but then landed in the middle of the bushes. Mrs. O'Leary was frantically trying to steer out of the way, and the car finally came to a stop against a snowdrift on the sidewalk.

At first, the only sound Patricia could hear was her own heart beating. Then she tried to sit up, without falling even deeper into the brittle hedge. Mrs. O'Leary's car door flew open, and she leaped out. Her face was very pale and she was trembling all over. She was trying to say something, but seemed to be too upset to speak.

"You know, I really *was* going to improve my attitude," Patricia said.

Mrs. O'Leary just stared at her.

Few things in life disappointed Patricia more than having a joke fall flat. With an effort, she pushed herself the rest of the way out of the hedge, hearing a tearing sound as she scrambled free.

"Well, shoot," she said, looking at a small rip in the sleeve of her Patriots jacket. She was very *fond* of her Patriots jacket.

"Patricia, I-I'm so sorry," Mrs. O'Leary stammered, her voice shaking. "Are you all right?"

Patricia nodded, wondering if her mother could discreetly sew the tear, or if a piece of blue electrical tape might do the trick.

"I-I was just going to offer you a ride home," Mrs. O'Leary stuttered. "I really didn't mean to — the ice — oh, this is terrible!"

Patricia grinned then, since it occurred to her that this narrowly-avoided accident probably meant that she wasn't going to get yelled at in class again anytime soon. That was an unexpected fringe benefit, which might almost make ripping her jacket worthwhile. "No, it's okay," she said. "Really. Is your car all right?"

Mrs. O'Leary blinked, and looked at her car. It was on the sidewalk, with the motor still running, but seemed to be undamaged. "Are you *sure* you're not hurt?" she asked.

If she made any sort of joke here, it would just be unkind. "Yes, I'm fine, thank you," Patricia said. "I'm pretty late, though, so I'd better head home now."

"Well then, please let me give you a ride," Mrs. O'Leary offered. "I'm really so very sorry."

The idea of getting into that particular car a minute or two after it had fish-tailed wildly across the street wasn't enticing. "Thank you, but I'm just going to go back and call my father," Patricia said, and gestured towards the school. "He's going to be wondering where I am."

"All right, but I'm going to come back with you," Mrs. O'Leary said. "I'll wait until I'm sure you're all set."

Patricia started to protest, but Mrs. O'Leary held up her hand.

"It's the least I can do," she said.

It didn't seem to be worth arguing, so Patricia just nodded. She stood *well* out of the way — poised to leap to safety again, if necessary — as Mrs. O'Leary moved her car off the sidewalk and parked very cautiously. Then they headed back towards the school entrance.

Patricia just hoped that her father would be able to come right over to pick her up. Somehow, it felt as though it had been an *unusually* long day.

Back at the house, Mr. Callahan had finished every storm preparation task he knew — and still, Patricia wasn't home yet. He immediately called the school, but the office assistant who answered assured him that all of the students had left for the day and that no student activities were scheduled in the building.

When he hung up the phone, Mr. Callahan looked at Santa Paws. "Okay, I am now officially worried about *both* of my children," he said.

Hearing the concern in his voice, the dog contributed a sympathetic woof, since he wasn't sure what else he could do to make Mr. Callahan feel better.

Mr. Callahan thought for a minute, scanned the list of frequently called numbers Mrs. Callahan had placed on the bulletin board, and dialed Patricia's friend Rachel's house. He let it ring at least eight times, but there was no answer. So he set the phone down and tried to remember if Patricia had made plans to go Christmas shopping, or anything else he might have forgotten.

In case she was walking home, he would go out and drive along her usual route. It wouldn't take long, and the sooner he found her, the better. The *last* thing he wanted was for her to be wandering around alone in an ice storm — especially after dark. Once Patricia was safe at home, he would only have to worry about *two* people, instead of three.

The dog watched uneasily as Mr. Callahan picked up his car keys and put on his coat and boots. This was very bad. Mr. Callahan should stay. The whole family should come home and they should all *stay*. That would be good.

The lights dimmed for a minute in a brown-out, and all of the kitchen appliances stopped running. Then, slowly, the electricity came back on, and the refrigerator kicked into its normal hum again. Mr. Callahan shook his head. People in Oceanport were *used* to having the power go out briefly during storms, but that didn't mean that it was ever *convenient*.

"I'm just going to go look for Patricia," he told Santa Paws. "I'll be right back, okay? Good dog."

Santa Paws had already started pacing apprehensively before Mr. Callahan even left the house. He went from room to room, cringing every time an especially hard gust of wind and ice pounded against the windows. Abigail came out from underneath the desk and mewed sadly at him.

Then, there was a sharp cracking sound outside as a huge tree limb crashed to the ground. They were both so startled that Abigail ran right back under the desk, and Santa Paws followed her.

When nothing else frightening happened, the dog ventured out — and resumed his restless patrol around the house.

If there was any trouble, he wanted to be ready to do anything he could to help!

*　*　*

Over at Eastman Junior High School, Gregory's team was playing surprisingly well against the Sharks. In fact, they had a two point lead at half-time! This probably had something to do with the fact that the Sharks' star power forward was home with the flu, but it would still be nice to win for once.

Gregory and his teammates were having trouble executing their new plays correctly, but their defense was strong and they scored a lot of points on fast-breaks. Oscar forgot and traveled a few times, because he would fade back like a quarterback waiting to pass, instead of remembering to dribble. "Hit the open man in the key, Oscar!" Coach Yancey kept telling him during time-outs. "Before the zone collapses on him." When Oscar finally gave up and looked at Gregory for a translation, Gregory said, "Throw me a slant pass when I cut across the middle." That made perfect sense to Oscar, who smiled and started doing just that.

The second half had just started when an official time-out was called, and the coaches and referees all huddled together.

"Sorry, boys," Coach Yancey said, when he returned to the sideline. "They're calling the game."

Oscar looked outraged. "Because we're *winning*?"

"Because the storm's really picking up out there, and they want us to head home before it gets any worse," Coach Yancey said. "We'll reschedule the game for sometime after the holidays."

"We'll pick up right where we left off, right?" Philip, the team's center, asked. "The score, I mean?"

Coach Yancey shook his head. "Sorry. It'll be a whole new game."

Gregory and the other Mariners were very disappointed by the news. They had been playing so well, and what were the odds that they would manage to do that again? Especially against *this* team. But they slouched off to the visiting team's locker-room, changed into their street clothes, and assembled back on the bus. Coach Yancey counted heads to make sure everyone was there, and then the driver, grouchy old Mr. Monroe, put the bus into gear with a harsh, grinding sound. Mr. Monroe was a retired Marine, and he thought that all students — no matter how old they were — should behave like well-trained, highly-motivated military recruits at all times. As a result, life as a junior high school bus driver was a constant letdown for him, and he spent most of his time grumbling and mumbling to himself.

"I can't believe it," Oscar said glumly. "We were going to *win* this one." Then his face brightened, and he waved to get Coach Yancey's attention. "Hey, Coach, can we stop at McDonald's?" That was the normal team tradition after games, win or lose.

"Not this time, Oscar," Coach Yancey said. "I'd rather just get you all back to the school."

"Even if we're really hungry?" Nathan, the scrawny team manager, asked. He was so small that he ate *constantly* in an attempt to grow. So far, it hadn't worked.

"Even if," Coach Yancey said. "Sorry."

The entire team sat in dejected silence. The only sounds were the windshield wipers beating back and forth, and the icy sleet hitting against the bus.

"Hey, wait!" Abdul, the second-string shooting guard, said, as he dug through his knapsack. "I've got band candy!"

"All right!" someone yelled. "Band candy!"

At least half the team exchanged high fives, and there was a general atmosphere of celebration.

"Let's have some quiet, ya little weevils!" Mr. Monroe bellowed. "I'm trying to drive here."

They were all — including Coach Yancey — a little bit afraid of Mr. Monroe, so everyone immediately began whispering instead of yelling. Abdul passed out overpriced and undersized bags of chocolate-nut candy.

"Don't you have to account for all of that candy later on, Abdul?" Coach Yancey asked in a low voice.

"Probably, yeah," Abdul said without much concern.

"Well, maybe you should have everyone write their names down first," Coach Yancey suggested, "or — "

"We're a team, Coach," Abdul said. "I trust my *team*."

Instead of arguing further, Coach Yancey just helped himself to some candy. Besides, he was hungry, too.

Gregory looked at the small piece of chocolate in his hand. Band candy *was* always amazingly expensive — and usually sort of stale and odd. "What do you think, is this about five dollars worth?" he asked Oscar.

Oscar nodded, and ate three dollars worth in one bite.

"Would you like some candy, Mr. Monroe?" Abdul asked politely. "To help you concentrate?"

Mr. Monroe glared at him in the rear view mirror. "Whatsa matter? Can't you see I'm driving, kid?"

"Yes, sir," Abdul said. "No excuse, sir."

Since that was an excellent imitation of a gung-ho military recruit, most of the team laughed.

"The power lines look pretty cool," Oscar said, pointing out the window at the icicles forming on the wires.

"Yeah, but I hope they don't break." Gregory crunched another two dollars worth of candy. "Remember the hurricane that time? It was like, four days before we got the power back."

"That was really boring," Oscar said. "I thought my brother was going to die without his video games." He paused. "I actually wasn't so happy, either."

Gregory hadn't liked it much himself, for that matter. "You should see Patricia if she can't get on the Internet for a couple of hours. She turns into this total maniac."

"That could be scary," Oscar said thoughtfully.

Gregory nodded. Patricia was nothing, if not addicted to being online. Their parents had finally had to break down and put in a second phone line, so that they could occasionally *receive* telephone calls.

"The worst Delia and Todd — " who were Oscar's little sister and brother — "ever do is stamp their feet and maybe cry a little," Oscar said.

Gregory tried to remember if he had ever seen Patricia stamp her foot. Mostly, she just narrowed her eyes and looked threatening. Since Gregory was bigger than she was now, their fights were never physical anymore, because Gregory liked to play fair — and Patricia was no fool. If she really got on his nerves, his current strategy was to look annoyed and say, snidely, "Oh, you're too *thin* to hit." Even though Patricia really liked being thin, that always infuriated her for some reason. Which, as strategies went, made it a superior weapon!

In the end, though, he was mainly happy that he had a sister who was so totally, irrefutably *cool*. He figured that it helped improve his own reputation, considerably.

Oscar gazed out the window as the sleet fell even harder. "Boy, I'm glad I'm not driving."

"Me, too," Gregory said. "It's looking really icy out there."

From where they were sitting, they could hear Mr. Monroe grumbling away, but he didn't sound any more crabby than usual. The road they were on was full of curves and Mr. Monroe seemed to be holding onto the steering wheel very tightly. The storm was so fierce now that there wasn't any other traffic on the road, so at least they didn't have to worry about other cars. The old Kenyon Bridge was just up ahead, rising over a deep watery channel leading inland from the ocean.

"Want to hear a science fun-fact?" Oscar asked.

"Not really," Gregory said. He enjoyed science, but still. "I mean, like, we're on *vacation*."

The bus wheels clattered as they started over the bridge.

"No, this is a good one," Oscar assured him. "I saw it on the Discovery Channel. When it's cold out, bridges freeze a whole lot faster than — "

Before he could finish his sentence, the bus suddenly began gliding off to the right. The side scraped noisily against the steel bridge supports, and then the bus bounced off and veered sharply in the other direction. Mr. Monroe tried to get control of the wheel, but the bus seemed to have a mind of its own.

Gregory and Oscar exchanged scared looks, and then braced themselves against the back of the seat in front of them.

It didn't seem possible, but they were about to crash!

6

Everyone started yelling at once. The bus swerved back and forth, first careening off one side of the bridge and then, the other. Equipment was flying all over the place, and people were being thrown out of their seats. It seemed to take forever, but Gregory didn't have time to think about anything more complicated than trying to hold on.

The bus skidded off the end of the bridge, burst through the guardrail, and rolled down the icy embankment. They landed in the frozen marsh below with a loud crunch. Then, as the bus finally came to a stop in the mire, it was absolutely silent inside.

Gregory found himself lying in the aisle, somewhere in the middle of a pile of his stunned teammates.

"Everyone all right?" Coach Yancey asked hoarsely. "Anyone hurt?"

There was no answer at first.

"Are we hurt?" Oscar asked Gregory. "I can't tell."

"I can't, either." Gregory carefully pulled his legs free and tried to climb onto the nearest seat.

The bus had landed at a steep angle, although luckily, it hadn't tipped all the way over. Gregory braced his foot on the side of the seat to keep his balance. His other foot slipped and knocked against Philip's shoulder.

"Hey, watch it, Callahan!" Philip protested.

"Sorry," Gregory said, and adjusted his position.

Looking around in the very dim light, he could see that everyone else seemed to be moving, which he figured was a good sign. A fair number of his teammates were groaning, though, or saying, "Ow." *That* seemed like a bad sign. And Mr. Monroe, up front, was holding one hand to his forehead.

"Is anyone *hurt*?" Coach Yancey asked again, sounding almost frantic.

Everyone started answering at the same time, so it was hard to understand what they were saying.

"One at a time, ya maniacs!" Mr. Monroe bellowed. Then he winced and brought his other hand up to his head, too.

Gregory moved his arms and legs experimentally, turned his head to the left and the right, shrugged his shoulders, and then decided that he was fine. "I'm okay, Coach," he said. "You okay, Oscar?"

"Yeah," Oscar answered, sounding a little uncertain.

It turned out that they were all mostly just shaken up and bruised, but Nathan, Kurt, Harry, and Jethro each had more serious twists and strains, some of which might involve fractures. Kurt almost definitely had a broken ankle, and Jethro's elbow was dislocated. Coach Yancey fished around through the jumbled pile of knapsacks and equipment bags, looking for the team's first aid kit.

"They call the game *and* we crash?" someone — maybe Abdul — said gloomily. "That really stinks."

Since Mr. Monroe hadn't volunteered anything yet, Gregory made his way up front to find out if he was not hurt. He was muttering something grim about being surrounded by "demented munchkins." Gregory would have been worried about a serious head injury, but that was the sort of thing Mr. Monroe *always* said.

"Sir?" he asked, making a point of sounding extra-polite. "Are you okay, Mr. Monroe?"

"Banged up my noggin some, but no problem," Mr. Monroe said grumpily. "Now, give me some space, kid — I gotta go check the vehicle." He started to stand up, looked dizzy, and abruptly sat back down.

"We'll take care of it," Coach Yancey said. "I'll just go flag a car down, and — " His voice trailed off when he looked up at the deserted, icy road. In order to flag a car down, one had to drive *by*.

"Oscar and I can go find a house and use their phone," Gregory suggested.

"Who you going to call?" Philip asked. "Triple A?"

Gregory and Oscar gave that some thoughtful consideration. It sounded like a sensible choice.

"911," Coach Yancey said firmly. "We want to call 911. But I really don't feel right about sending you two — "

Kurt looked up from his swollen ankle. "You feel right *leaving* the rest of us here, Coach? With broken bones and all?"

"Well, no," Coach Yancey conceded. "But — "

"Coach, I've *done* this before," Gregory said. "And this is only the suburbs."

Everyone in town knew about the plane crash he had been in, and how he and Patricia and Santa Paws had been forced to cross miles over the White Mountains in the middle of a blizzard to find help for their injured Uncle Steve. Gregory never brought it up — he didn't like remembering the experience, and it also felt like bragging — but this was a good time to make an exception.

"Yeah, I guess you have," Coach Yancey said. "Okay, you two head out and find a telephone.

There are a few houses just up the road there. But, please be *very* careful." Then he sighed. "Frankly, I wish that dog of yours was here right now."

Gregory wished the exact same thing.

Patricia had called home from the main office at the junior high school, but the answering machine picked up. She left a message saying where she was, and asking one of her parents to come pick her up please whenever they got home.

"I'm happy to give you a ride, Patricia," Mrs. O'Leary said.

Patricia still wasn't eager to get into a car that did *quite* that much skidding. "It's okay. I honestly don't mind waiting."

Mrs. O'Leary put her hands on her hips. "Well, now, really. What happened outside was a fluke. I'm a perfectly competent driver."

"Oh, I know," Patricia said. Anyway, she *hoped* so. "But they're going to be coming over here soon to pick up my brother, anyway, so no problem."

When the vice principal, Mr. Weingarten, said that Patricia could wait in the office until her ride came, Mrs. O'Leary finally gave in. With one last profuse apology — and a stilted "have a happy holiday" exchange, she left.

"Well, now! It's certainly nice to have you here in this office for a reason unrelated to discipline,

Miss Callahan," Mr. Weingarten said with a big smile.

Patricia didn't get sent to the principal's office very often, but when it happened, it was usually quite complicated and unforgettable — for everyone involved. She didn't mention that she wouldn't still be at school in the first place, if she hadn't gotten detention today. "Yes, sir," she said. "It makes for a nice change."

From force of habit, she automatically sat in the row of metal seats designated for problem students, and then took a book out of her knapsack to pass the time.

"I'm guessing that's one of those Harry Potter books you kids enjoy so much," Mr. Weingarten said with his wide, hearty smile. He was a nice man, but sometimes he had a tendency to try just a little too hard to be "hip."

Patricia held up her book — *The Sound and the Fury* by William Faulkner. She was also reading a book about the Salem witch trials and another about strategies for the small investor, but she had left them both at home.

Mr. Weingarten's face fell. "Oh. Well — enjoy."

Patricia nodded and opened to the page where she had left her bookmark. She had been reading for ten or fifteen minutes when she heard her father's voice out in the hallway. She closed her book and went out to meet him.

Mr. Callahan looked very relieved when he

saw her. "There you are, Patricia! Where have you been?"

Her parents liked it when she and Gregory were honest. "Well, I sort of had, um, detention," Patricia said.

Mr. Callahan lifted his eyebrows. "Sort of?"

"It was pretty minor detention," Patricia said, in her own defense.

"Mrs. O'Leary again?" he guessed.

Patricia nodded, and then looked at him uncertainly. "Are you going to yell at me?"

"No," Mr. Callahan said, after a lengthy and pointed pause. "I'm going to give you a life lesson."

Patricia — almost — repressed a shudder. "This isn't going to be the 'honesty is the best policy' one, is it?" Her father had an endless supply of Life Lessons, which he sometimes referred to as "thematic arcs."

"No. This is the 'go along to get along' one," Mr. Callahan said. "Okay? It saves a lot of time."

"Like you and your editor this morning?" Patricia asked.

Mr. Callahan elected not to answer that question. "Why don't we just head home before that ice gets any worse," he said.

Patricia stuck her book back into her knapsack to protect it from the sleet. "Is Mom going to pick up Greg when his bus gets here?"

Mr. Callahan moved his jacket sleeve up so he

could look at his watch. "No, it's late enough so that we might as well wait for him." Seeing Mr. Weingarten come out of his office, Mr. Callahan motioned to get his attention. "Hi, Mark. When are you expecting the basketball team back?"

"About half an hour ago, now that you mention it," Mr. Weingarten said. "They ended up canceling the game because of the weather."

"*After* they got all the way over there?" Mr. Callahan asked.

Mr. Weingarten nodded. "And to make matters worse, they were *winning*."

"No wonder the other team wanted to cancel the game," Patricia said with a grin. Then she noticed her father's worried expression. "What's wrong, Dad?"

"Oh, I'm sure they just got held up," Mr. Callahan said, looking distracted. "Do you know what time they started back here, Mark?"

Mr. Weingarten was also looking concerned now. "No, but let me go find out."

"Do you think something happened?" Patricia asked, beginning to feel pretty uneasy herself.

"No," Mr. Callahan said quickly. "I'm sure they're perfectly fine."

But Patricia could tell that he really wasn't sure at all. "It's only two towns over. And Mr. Monroe's a really good driver."

"Absolutely," Mr. Callahan agreed without any

hesitation. "I'm sure they'll be here any second now."

Since he was avoiding her eyes, Patricia knew that he was just trying to keep her from worrying. However, if that was his goal, unfortunately he was already too late.

When Mr. Weingarten came back out, his hearty smile was completely gone. "They, uh, they left over an hour ago," he said.

"But, wait, that means — " Patricia stopped in the middle of her sentence. She knew perfectly well what it meant.

Gregory's bus was missing!

Back at the house, Santa Paws was still roaming restlessly from room to room. Abigail sprawled out on the living room rug, hoping that he might roughhouse with her, but the dog ignored her. He had other things on his mind.

He stood at the backdoor for a while, alert for any sound which might mean his family had come home. But all he could hear was the howling wind and tree branches snapping off all over the neighborhood.

Abigail joined him in the kitchen. She found an empty paper cup on the counter and knocked it onto the floor. Then she rolled it away, pounced on it, and swatted it across the linoleum again.

Santa Paws was so busy concentrating on

what was going on outside that he didn't even notice her energetic game. A draft of cold air was blowing in through the tiny gap at the bottom right corner of the door frame. He couldn't smell anything unfamiliar, but the odor of the ocean was much stronger than usual and the snapped tree limbs were adding a distinct fragrance of fresh sap to the air.

Feeling lonely and bored, Abigail came over and rubbed against the dog's front legs, purring loudly. Santa Paws didn't encourage her, but he didn't show his teeth or move away, either. He loved Abigail, but he wished she would stop being so silly, with such a horrible storm going on outside. This was a very bad time for playing games! He just couldn't pay attention to her right now.

He could hear a strange squeaking sound, which seemed to be coming from the old maple tree in the front yard. He dashed out of the kitchen towards the living room. The tree was right outside the bay windows, and he wanted to check that squeaking more closely.

It was too dark to see clearly, but the branches of the tree seemed to be whipping wildly from side to side. No, the entire *tree* seemed to be moving. It was bending back and forth as though it might fall right down!

The dog could feel strong pressure in his ears from the growing power of the storm, and the bay windows were shaking so hard that he was afraid that they might burst open. He whimpered a little in spite of himself, and shook his head and lowered his ears to try and reduce the pressure inside them. It hurt!

Abigail's ears must have been painful, too, because they were bent back along the side of her head, and she wouldn't even come *in* to the living room. She was also meowing unhappily. The dog decided that she had the right idea, and he began backing out of the room. He stayed low to the floor, almost crawling.

There was a terrifying, shrieking crack out in the yard, and the dog stopped short in alarm. What was *that*? What a loud noise! Why didn't it stop?

The oak tree, weakened from decades of nor'-easters and hurricanes, had just splintered in half. And now one huge section was crashing straight towards the house!

The branches scraped across the windows, and then the glass shattered from the force of the falling tree. Part of it landed on the roof with a loud crunch, and the rest of the tree came plunging right into the living room!

The dog yelped in fear, and leaped backwards into the hall. He landed on top of Abigail, who had flattened on the floor to protect herself. She meowed in protest and squirmed free. In a panic, they both ran into the den as fast as they could.

A tree! It had come right into their *house*. It almost seemed to be attacking them!

The dog wanted to hide under Mr. Callahan's desk, but he could feel the wind and cold air seeping inside from the destroyed windows in the living room. He panted nervously for a minute, and then ventured back out to the hall. He peeked around the side of the doorway, and was very upset to see that the tree was still there. Trees weren't *supposed* to come into the house like that. Not ever. The Callahans were going to think that he was a very bad dog.

The branches were filling most of the space left by the broken windows, so not much sleet was falling into the house yet, but the temperature in the room was dropping quickly. The dog was afraid that *another* tree might come down on top of him, but he forced himself to move a few steps closer and investigate.

Something brushed against his back leg, and he jumped in fear. It was only Abigail, and she gave him a little whack with her paw to show her displeasure at his dramatic reaction. The dog felt scared and shaky, so he sat down to do some more panting. Once he felt calmer, he got up again.

He approached the tree and nosed at the ice-covered branches. They didn't move, and he relaxed a little.

Abigail thought trees were fun, so she started climbing on the branches. But the ice was so slippery that she fell off and landed in a jumbled heap on the rug. She rolled to her feet, shook her fur disdainfully, and then retreated out to the hall to wash — and attempt to recover her wounded dignity.

Evelyn had crept cautiously downstairs to see why there had been such a terrible crash. She took one look at the tree and went right back up to the linen closet. It was very warm in there, sleeping all curled up in a nest of clean towels, and she had *no* intention of coming out again until the storm was over.

The dog was still in the living room. He sat back on his haunches, perplexed. Should he stay here on guard? Should he go back out to the kitchen and wait? It would be much easier if the Callahans were here, because they would say things like "Stay" or "Come," and then he would know what he should do.

But where *were* the Callahans? It was much too scary for them to be outside right now. What if they were hurt? What if they *needed* him? What if they were lost? They *must* be lost, if they weren't home yet.

The dog got up and paced anxiously in front of the smashed windows. He wasn't supposed to go outside unless the Callahans said it was okay.

Most of the time, one of them even came outside *with* him. Sometimes he even wore a leash! Leaving on his own was against all of the rules.

But he knew that he could wiggle past those branches and get out of the house. It might be bad if he did that, but they should *be* here. He was *sure* that they should be home by now. He should check on them.

The dog stayed in the living room for one last indecisive second. Then he vaulted up onto the branches and began to make his way clumsily towards the windows. He lost his balance a couple of times, but finally managed to shove through the opening and jumped outside into the roaring storm.

He was going to go find his family!

7

The dog stood by the fallen tree for a minute to think. The storm had already done a lot of damage, and the yard was so strewn with huge branches that it looked completely different. In fact, he felt a little disoriented. Had the whole *town* changed this way, or was it only happening at the Callahans' house?

There was a thud — and a small squeak of dismay — as Abigail landed on the ice behind him. Abigail *always* arrived on *noisy* little cat feet. When the dog jumped out the window, she had concluded that whatever Santa Paws was doing, she wanted to do, too. But now that she was actually outside in the sleet and freezing rain, she was having second thoughts.

The dog was very upset to see her. First of all, she was too small, and the storm was too dangerous for her to be out here. And if she *did* come, she would just get in his way. For one thing, she was a big baby about cold weather, and started shivering and complaining if she felt even an imaginary chill. She also tired easily, wouldn't be able to keep up — and had an *incredibly* short attention span, so she would lose interest in what they were doing before they even got a block away from the house.

He barked sharply at her in an attempt to encourage her to go back inside through the broken windows.

Abigail paid no attention to this. Instead, she started practicing how to keep her balance on the ice-crusted snow. It was hard, but she liked a challenge, even if the ice felt unpleasant against her paws.

The dog growled softly, and tried to herd her in the direction of the tree — and the safety of the house. Abigail just turned her back on him, twitched her tail in his face, and continued delicately picking her way across the ice.

The dog gave up, since he had never — not even once! — won an argument with a cat. *Any* cat. He decided to go to the driveway, and see if he could trace the scent of Mr. Callahan's Buick from there. Cars were very hard to follow, because they all smelled so much alike on the roads, but he could at least give it a try.

He sprang over the gate and went into a controlled slide when he hit the ground. Abigail attempted to do the same thing, but she crashed right into a snowbank with another alarmed squeak. She struggled to her feet, and then gave each paw in turn a persnickety shake. The dog hoped that she would come to her senses now and go back inside, but he also knew that she was too stubborn for that. So he just pretended that she wasn't even there.

The sleet was swirling around violently, and each little ice pellet *hurt* when it hit them. The dog was feeling less sure about his idea to go off searching for his family in this terrible weather, but the thought that they might *need* him was uppermost in his mind. That was much more important than his own comfort.

All he could tell for sure was that Mr. Callahan's car had turned right when he pulled out of the driveway. Beyond that, there wasn't much of a trail. Still, it was a place to start.

He began trotting down the street, hoping to catch even the faintest familiar scent. The road was covered with ice, and tree branches had landed in unexpected places. It was a winter obstacle course!

Behind him, Abigail allowed herself one mournful, self-pitying mew. Then she puffed up her fur to make herself feel brave, and scampered after him.

The dog was determined to keep looking for his family until he had found every single one of them. No storm, no matter how fierce, was going to be enough to stop *him*.

The school bus was so badly tilted at the bottom of the embankment that Gregory and Oscar couldn't get the front door open. Coach Yancey and a couple of their teammates helped them climb through the emergency exit in the back. They both jumped out, landing knee-deep in the only partially-frozen marsh. Actually, in Oscar's case, it was more like *hip*-deep.

"Maybe he should have sent someone taller," Oscar said, looking down.

"I could go by myself," Gregory offered, even though the idea of braving the storm alone was pretty intimidating.

Oscar shook his head vehemently. "What, and let you get all the glory? Not a chance, bud."

Gregory grinned, and they began trudging towards the steep slope leading to the road. The water smelled strongly of the sea, and was incredibly cold. Every step was an effort, because they kept sinking into the icy muck. The marsh grass was rigid with ice and broke off whenever they tried to use it to pull themselves along.

"I wonder if rice paddies felt like this," Oscar said, his teeth chattering a little. His father had served in Vietnam, and Oscar had always been intensely curious about what that must have been like. His father was proud of his service — but he didn't talk about it very often.

"It was really *hot* there, though," Gregory said, shivering. "Right?"

"Far as I know, yeah." Oscar yanked one high-top out of the partially-frozen mud with a loud sucking sound. He had to pull so hard that it almost came right off his foot! "I guess this is totally different."

"No war going on, either," Gregory pointed out.

"So far," Oscar said, sounding very pessimistic.

They both fell about six times on their way up the steep embankment. By the time they made it up to the road, they were wet, frustrated, and *cold*. It would have been nice if a car had been conveniently driving past, but the road was empty in both directions.

Oscar glanced down at the stranded bus. "You know, crashing was really scary and all, but I'm kind of thinking we were *really* lucky."

Gregory wasn't sure he *wanted* to think about it. There were just too many scary possibilities. "Um, yeah," he said, looking away. "But let's just, you know, hurry up and find a house or something."

They had only gone about a hundred feet down the road when all of the streetlights blinked out at once. It was a shock to find themselves in complete darkness.

Gregory felt a second of panic, but then took a

deep breath. "Whoa. Okay. Okay, no big deal."

"Power must have gone out," Oscar said.

"Yeah," Gregory agreed. It wasn't really a surprise, considering how bad the storm was, but it *was* pretty spooky.

Their eyes were starting to adjust a little, and they started walking again. Being in the dark made it that much harder to keep from falling on the ice every other step.

"Made you think about the plane, didn't it," Oscar said unexpectedly.

The crash. "Yeah," Gregory admitted. "It sort of freaked me out, a little."

"Don't worry, Greg — it freaked *all* of us out," Oscar said. "I mean, you know, it was *scary*."

"We could have flipped over," Gregory said, hearing his voice shake. "We could have fallen into really deep water, we could have — all kinds of awful things. And we could have really gotten *hurt*." Or worse.

"But we're okay," Oscar said. "Mr. Monroe did a good job keeping us from turning over or anything."

Gregory nodded. Yes. They were lucky. No question about it. But it had still scared him pretty badly.

"Do you think about the plane a lot?" Oscar asked curiously.

Gregory shook his head. "Not really. Especially since Uncle Steve got off his cane and all, so we don't have to remember the whole thing every time we look at him. I just — have dreams about it sometimes." *Bad* dreams.

"I wonder if — " Oscar slipped and landed hard on the street, his hands taking the brunt of the fall. "Ouch."

Gregory helped him back up. "You all right?"

"Yeah." Oscar brushed off some of the ice and snow. "You think Patricia has nightmares about it, too?"

"Probably," Gregory said. Did she? He had no idea, really. Mostly she claimed that she only dreamed about George Clooney — and sometimes, a younger version of Gene Hackman. "Although I can't see her *telling* anyone, if she did. Except for Rachel, maybe." He shrugged. "I don't know. Sometimes I'm not sure if all *girls* are weird, or just Patricia, know what I mean?"

Oscar laughed. "Yeah, she's probably not the best test case, for figuring out girls in general. After growing up with her, either they're *all* going to want to date you, or else *none* of them are."

Gregory had to laugh, too. "Thanks, Oscar. That makes me feel a whole lot better about things."

"That was the plan," Oscar said cheerfully.

There were three houses off to the side of the road, but with the power out, it was hard to tell if anyone was home.

"What do you think?" Gregory asked.

Oscar pointed at the middle house, where there seemed to be a bobbing light moving past one of the upstairs windows. "That one. Unless, you know, it's just *haunted*."

Gregory laughed again. "You really *do* know just what to say. You've got the gift, man."

"Well, hey," Oscar said, and ducked his head modestly.

They made their way up the treacherously slick front walk, and Oscar pushed the doorbell. They waited for a minute, and then Oscar tried the doorbell a second time.

"I guess the ghost doesn't want company," he said.

Gregory gave him a playful push, but with the ice underfoot, Oscar promptly fell down.

"Oh." Gregory looked guilty. "Sorry."

Oscar climbed to his feet with a long-suffering sigh. "No problem. Keep trying and I'll let you know when I break something." He reached out for the doorbell again, and then stopped. "Are doorbells electric?"

Gregory closed his eyes. *Boy*, were they stupid. "Yes."

"Thought so," Oscar said, and took his glove off so that he could knock on the door instead.

After a minute, the door opened and a flashlight pointed at them.

"Um, hi," Gregory said, lifting his hand to

block the brightness of the beam. Because of the light in his eyes, he couldn't even tell if the person who had opened the door was a man or a woman — or, for that matter, a *ghost*. "Our bus just crashed over by the bridge, and we were wondering if you could please call the police for us?"

The flashlight beam lowered enough so that they could see an elderly man with white hair and thick glasses. "Sure, boys," he said. "I think my telephone's still working. Is anyone up there hurt?"

Gregory nodded. "I'm pretty sure our driver has a concussion, and Kurt broke his ankle and everything. I guess we need ambulances, too."

The man walked over to an end table in his front hall and picked up a portable telephone. Just as he started to dial, he paused, looking curiously at Gregory. "You seem awfully familiar, son. Do I know your parents?"

Gregory squinted at him in the glow from the flashlight, and then remembered when they had met. Last spring, this same man had been fishing off the town pier when he dropped his wallet in the water by mistake. Without even being asked, Santa Paws had promptly jumped in and fetched it for him.

"Not really, sir," he answered, "but I think you know my dog, Santa Paws."

The man nodded with recognition. "Of course!

Wonderful dog, that Santa Paws. A credit to us all." Then he remembered something else. "Is your father that nice writer fellow who always shows up at the diner in his slippers?"

There was no way around it — Oceanport was a *small* town. "Yes, sir," Gregory said.

"Well, how about that," the elderly man said, sounding pleased. "Nice to meet you." Then he dialed 911. "Hello?" he said when the dispatcher picked up. "I want to report an accident."

Gregory and Oscar exchanged triumphant smiles. They had done it! Now help was only minutes away.

Patricia and Mr. Callahan were still sitting in the main office at the junior high school, waiting for news. Other parents had arrived, expecting to pick up their sons, and they were just as upset when they discovered that no one knew where the bus was — or if the team was okay. Some of them were making panicked phone calls, some were planning to go out and search for the bus, and everyone else was either just sitting glumly in the row of disciplinary chairs or pacing up and down the corridors. Mr. Callahan had already called the police station to make sure that sector cars would be looking for the missing bus while they patrolled. Things at the station were starting to get so hectic because of the weather, that he hadn't been able to speak to Uncle Steve directly.

Patricia kept trying to think of something distracting to say, but her mind was a blank. Her brother was probably fine — but what if he *wasn't*? She liked to give him a certain amount of grief, but that didn't mean that she still wasn't crazy about him. Gregory was so steady, and dependable, and easygoing, and — he was just about her favorite person in the world. If anything bad happened to him, she wouldn't know what to do.

"I'm getting cellphones for the whole family," Mr. Callahan said decisively. "That way, we can actually keep track of one another."

Under any other circumstances, Patricia would have been elated to hear that idea — her own cellphone! — but right now, she was too worried.

"Maybe beepers, too," Mr. Callahan said, thinking aloud.

Patricia decided to break the tension with a little joke. "We also could have microchips implanted." After they had recovered Santa Paws last year, their veterinarian, Dr. Kasanofsky, had put one in the loose skin on his neck — just in case.

To her horror, Mr. Callahan actually seemed to be *considering* the idea.

"Joke, Dad," she said.

He looked startled, but then nodded. "Right. I suppose that would be — impractical."

"Just a little, yeah," Patricia said.

They sat silently after that, waiting to hear the office telephone ring with some news — or for the bus to pull up in front of the building as though nothing unusual had happened.

"So," Mr. Callahan said brightly. "How was school?"

Patricia had to check his expression first, to make sure that he was serious. "Oh. It was, um, swell."

Her father nodded, apparently wanting her to elaborate.

"Uh, I learned a great deal," Patricia said. "Things that I can probably apply throughout the rest of my — " From where she was sitting, she could see a police car arrive in front of the school, followed by a second, and then a *third*.

Her father saw the police cars too, and slowly stood up as though he were expecting bad news.

The back door of the first car opened and someone stepped out, almost losing his balance on the icy curb.

It was Gregory!

8

Not that she was glad to see him, but Patricia was the first one out the door to meet the police cars. She maybe even *ran*. Mr. Callahan and the rest of the parents — and Mr. Weingarten — were quick to follow her.

"Everything okay?" she asked. "What happened?"

Gregory shrugged casually. "The bus crashed," he said. "So the police had to drive us back."

"Yeah, you should have seen it — we went right off the side of the bridge! Totally out of control!" Oscar said, and then waved at his mother. "Hi, Mom."

"That bus is *toast*," Abdul added, and then smiled at his father hurrying to greet him. "Hey, Dad, I sold all my band candy!"

Gregory and Oscar exchanged guilty looks.

"Um, Dad, can I maybe borrow some money to pay for all the band candy I ate?" Gregory asked.

"Me, too, Mom," Oscar said meekly to his mother.

"Better make that a blank check," Patricia advised, as her father blinked and reached for his wallet.

The parents whose children had been taken straight to the hospital were very upset when they heard that their sons had been hurt in the crash, but relieved when they were assured that none of the injuries appeared to be serious.

As Gregory, Patricia, and their father headed for the Buick, Gregory was still acting very nonchalant. But once he got inside, his face began to look a little green.

"Busy being cool in front of the guys?" Patricia asked.

Gregory nodded, snapped on his seatbelt, and slumped down in the backseat with his eyes closed. Now that it was all over, he just wanted to go home and lie down for a while. There was part of a leftover apple pie in the refrigerator — if his father hadn't eaten it already — and a piece of that might be nice, too.

"Well, I'm just grateful that you're here, and in one piece, and — well, 'grateful' pretty much covers it, actually," Mr. Callahan said.

As he turned on the engine, the CD player immediately began to blare Frank Sinatra belting out "Fly Me to the Moon." Patricia and Gregory groaned and put their hands over their ears.

"Sorry," Mr. Callahan said, and turned the volume down. "But, that was an alternate take, you know. Very rare."

Gregory and Patricia had absolutely no sensible response to this.

Mr. Callahan drove extremely slowly, but the car still lost traction a couple of times. Whenever it happened, Gregory sucked in his breath, and Patricia reached back over the front seat to pat his arm.

"If it makes you feel better, Mrs. O'Leary almost ran me over before," she said.

Her father turned to stare at her.

"Oops," Patricia said, and faced forward again.

Gregory shook his head. "I know she doesn't like you, but — wow."

"Why didn't you think to mention this to me, Patricia?" Mr. Callahan asked.

Patricia smiled sweetly at him. "Mention what?"

When they drove up their street, they could see that the power was still on — but a tree had fallen onto the roof, and seemingly inside the house, too.

Gregory gasped. "Whoa! Look at *that*!"

"Well — " Mr. Callahan stopped, as though he might have been about to swear. "Gosh. Darn. Shucks."

"What's your deductible, Dad?" Patricia asked.

He just looked at her, and then parked the car.

Patricia fell as she opened the gate, and Gregory and Mr. Callahan almost did, too, when they tried to help her up.

"I don't like this storm," she said, rubbing her bruised elbow. "I don't like anything about it."

Gregory went ahead to examine the splintered trunk of the old oak. He shook his head sadly. "I used to *climb* this tree."

"Used to fall out of it a lot, too," Patricia said.

That was true, but it had still always been a great old tree. Then Gregory thought of something. "Hey, Santa Paws and the cats must have been really scared! We'd better go make sure they're okay."

To their horror, once they got inside, they couldn't find *any* of the animals. Gregory hadn't cried when the bus crashed, but he was *very* close to crying now.

"They didn't just steal Santa Paws this time," he said miserably. "They came and stole *all* of them."

The two thieves had actually been arrested long ago — and convicted of dog-napping and assorted other criminal charges. "They're both still in jail, Greg," Mr. Callahan said, resting a gentle hand on his shoulder. "No one came in here. The cats are probably just hiding somewhere, and Santa Paws — " Santa Paws was too *big* to hide successfully, so there was no way of pretending that they had just conveniently overlooked him during their frantic search of the house. "I'm sure he's just — well — "

"I know where he is," Patricia said quietly.

Gregory and Mr. Callahan stared at her, their expressions somewhere between skepticism and hope.

"He's out looking for *us*," she said.

Her brother and father didn't bother arguing with that — because once she had said it aloud, they knew she was right.

Santa Paws and Abigail had ranged about a mile away from the house as Santa Paws explored each and every street thoroughly. Abigail's paws were cold, so she was getting sulky and lagging behind him. The dog was not sympathetic, since he had not exactly invited her along on this expedition. Mainly, he was upset that they had found no sign of the Callahans so far. Where *were* they? Should they go home and check again, or should they keep looking? He just didn't know what to do.

They were trotting down Hawthorne Street, when the dog heard unhappy whimpering. He stopped short, and Abigail bumped right into him. She hissed and gave his hip a hard swat with her paw. Since the dog's coat was fairly frozen, he didn't even feel her claws — and didn't bother reacting in any way. Abigail seemed disappointed by his lack of response and hauled her paw back to take another shot at him. The dog sensed the blow coming and neatly side-stepped out of the way just in time. Disgruntled about having swung and missed, Abigail sat down and began to wash the paw as though that had been her original intention.

The whimpering seemed to be coming from the mailbox on the street corner. Santa Paws rushed over and found a small, quivering puppy crouched down underneath it in an attempt to avoid the sleet. The puppy was a young spaniel mix who belonged to a family who lived about two blocks away. He was very mischievous and liked to squeeze under the fence surrounding his yard whenever possible. Then he would romp joyfully around the neighborhood until someone in his family came and found him. The storm had frightened him, though, and he was convinced that this time, he was lost forever.

Santa Paws barked a quick greeting, and the puppy wagged his tail shyly. Abigail came over and hissed at him, but neglected to scratch him since he looked so bedraggled and pathetic. Santa Paws had seen this puppy before while he was on walks with Gregory, so he knew exactly where he lived. He firmly nudged the puppy to his feet and began to escort him home.

A car drove down the street at one point, and the dog ushered both the puppy and Abigail safely out of the way until it had passed them.

Then he resumed leading the puppy home. The hole in the fence was too small for Santa Paws to crawl underneath, but the puppy squirmed through happily and began to gambol around his backyard.

The dog knew that he couldn't just leave, because that goofy puppy would probably run right out again ten minutes later. He really didn't like it when he had to perform the same rescues *twice*. So he ran over to the fence's gate and began to bark as loudly as he could. Abigail was beyond bored by this entire episode, but she ambled vaguely after him.

The backdoor of the house opened, and an older woman came outside. She wasn't wearing a coat, and she started shivering immediately.

"Well, there you are, Nelson!" she said, ecstatic to have her puppy back home in one piece. She scooped him up into her arms and gave the top of his head a big kiss. "We were *very* worried about you."

Santa Paws barked a few times, hoping she would understand that the puppy had to *stay* inside until the storm was over. In fact, as far as he was concerned, maybe the puppy ought to learn how to stay in *general*.

The woman walked over to the gate to see who had barked. "Well, hello, Santa Paws," she said, with a wide smile. "Did you bring Nelson home for us? Thank you! What a good dog you are!"

Good! Yay! The dog wagged his tail.

The woman noticed Abigail lounging around behind him, and beamed at her, too. "And who's your little friend, I wonder? Well, you're a good, smart cat, whoever you are."

Abigail yawned and turned to look in the opposite direction.

"Well, you two hurry home now," the woman advised them. "This weather is just frightful!" She turned to go back into the house. "Good night, Santa Paws — and thank you again!"

The dog waited until he saw the door close before starting down the street to continue his search for the Callahans. Abigail looked deeply apathetic, but then gave in and darted after him. They had only gone another few blocks when they heard a faint voice calling out from someplace close by.

"Help!" the voice wailed. "Someone, please help me!"

The dog stopped in his tracks. It was going to be very hard to find his family, if he kept having so many interruptions! But he spun around at once and followed the sound of the voice. If there was one word he knew well, it was the word *"Help."*

After her teachers' meeting, Mrs. Callahan had driven directly over to the mall, which was on the outskirts of town. She noticed that the roads were, indeed, a tad slick, but she was too busy thinking about what was left on her Christmas list to give the weather conditions much attention.

The mall was crowded with other last-minute shoppers, and Mrs. Callahan waited in line after line, in store after store. At this rate, she would be lucky to get home in time to *eat* supper, forget helping prepare it.

Once or twice, the lights in the various stores dimmed, and everyone in the lines would make jokes about wishing they had completed all of their shopping on the Internet weeks ago. The general consensus was that the weather was no match for the power of determined consumers and the holiday shopping season.

Mrs. Callahan thought about calling home to let the family know that her excursion was taking much longer than she had expected, but each payphone seemed to have a very long line. In any case, she assumed she would be done soon.

An hour and a half later, that assumption seemed overly optimistic. After waiting in one final line with two pairs of wacky slippers she couldn't resist buying for a certain eccentric writer, she decided that she would just have to finish the rest of her shopping the next day. She disliked shopping on Christmas Eve, but yet again this year, she would be doing so.

The parking lot was so slick that people were

having trouble getting to their cars without falling. Mrs. Callahan copied the idea she saw a couple of other people using, and stood on the back of a shopping cart like a ten-year-old in order to glide over to her car. This technique was quite successful, and in all honesty, entertaining enough to make her want to do it again. However, she was running late enough as it was.

The station wagon was encased in a thin layer of fresh ice, which she had to chip away with her keys in order to open the door. Then she had to run the car heater for a while, so that the windshield would defrost enough for her to be able to scrape *that* sheen of ice away, too. It was beginning to seem like a terrible night to have to be out on the road, and she wished that the mall were closer to her house. But it wasn't, so she just took a deep breath and put the car into gear.

She saw two fender-benders happen up in front of her before she even got out of the parking lot. There were also cars sliding all over the place on the main road, no matter how slowly people tried to drive. One car coasted helplessly right through a red-light, and smashed into a pick-up truck coming from the other direction. Neither driver was hurt, but both cars were badly damaged and blocking the road.

Traffic began to back up as everyone waited for tow trucks to clear away the disabled cars, and for the police to arrive to direct traffic. After ten minutes, Mrs. Callahan began to get impatient, so she turned off onto a side road. It would be much faster to detour around all of the main routes, and avoid other cars as much as possible.

The ice was treacherous, but the car's snow tires maintained reasonably good traction — which came as a relief. Unfortunately, she didn't have any chains, but they would have helped, too. Mrs. Callahan drove through a couple of neighborhoods which were completely dark, so the power must be starting to go out in various parts of town. She hoped that her house hadn't been affected by the outages, and her first worry was about all of the Christmas food in the refrigerator and the possibility of its spoiling. It would be a shame to waste all of the food — and have to do even more shopping to replace it.

There was a huge branch blocking the street in front of her, and she had to divert to yet another back route. Maybe this *was* a pretty serious storm! The wind was howling so loudly that she could even hear it inside the car with all of the windows shut, and her windshield wipers could barely keep up with the violent gusts of sleet. There was no traffic on the back roads, but somehow that isolation made the driving seem even more stressful than it might have been otherwise.

Looking for a pleasant distraction, Mrs. Callahan flipped the radio on, but every single station seemed to be exclusively airing dire weather bulletins and travel advisories. So much for happy holiday tunes. Since she already *knew* that the weather was terrible, she turned the radio off again and drove in silence.

The neighborhood she was passing through now was a brand-new housing development. Most of the homes hadn't even been completed — or sold, and no one had moved in yet. Even an endless traffic jam seemed more appealing than such a lonely road, so Mrs. Callahan started to turn around and make her way back to one of the main routes.

There was a strange shattering sound off to her right, and she couldn't imagine what it might be. But she put her foot gently on the brakes, just in case. There was a huge dark shape coming towards her, and Mrs. Callahan realized that it was a giant tree falling. She pressed her foot down on the accelerator and tried to swerve out of the way, but it was too late.

The tree landed right on top of her car!

9

Santa Paws had very little trouble tracking the call for help to a driveway halfway down the block. A man was lying on his back, gasping for breath and clutching his chest. It was Mr. Spiegel, who had come out to shovel a path behind his car before the ice got any thicker. As a rule, he never exercised, so the stress and the strain of shoveling had been too much for him. There was a terrible crushing pain in his chest, and he was almost sure that he was having a heart attack.

Mr. Spiegel looked up blearily to see a large German shepherd mix and a small black cat standing above him.

"You're Santa Paws, aren't you," he said, his voice weak. "Please help me. I need a doctor."

Santa Paws knew that *something* was wrong with this man, but he didn't know what it was. But he had learned long ago that whenever he was stuck for an answer, he just had to find a nice person to help him out. He pawed the man's shoulder gently, woofed once, and then trotted off to locate someone to take care of this situation for him.

When Abigail started to accompany him, the dog used his paw to propel her back in the direction of the man. He should *not* be left alone. Abigail meowed angrily, but she *was* feeling tired. Maybe she could stay next to this man and have a brief rest, while they waited for Santa Paws to come back. She liked naps a lot better than officious little errands, anyway. In her opinion, Santa Paws could be rather irritating and single-minded when he was off on a mission. She would just as soon skip the usual hectic sprint around the neighborhood, frankly.

Mr. Spiegel did his best to take deep breaths. He was very frightened by the symptoms he was having, and it was hard not to panic.

The freezing rain was so chilly that Abigail burrowed up underneath Mr. Spiegel's coat for warmth. Then she curled up and went to sleep, purring quietly. Mr. Spiegel was surprised that such a small sound could be so comforting, and he made an effort to concentrate on the warm rumbling of the little cat's purr. It made him feel a tiny bit better, although he was still extremely scared.

The dog ran to three different houses, barking his deepest bark in front of each one. There didn't seem to be anyone home, and he had to sit down for a few seconds to think of a better plan. That nice man back there was sick, and needed his help right away! He couldn't waste time!

Santa Paws shifted his weight indecisively. When he barked at doors, people almost always came outside to see what was wrong. He *depended* on that. But this time, he would have to — *make something up?* If only Gregory and Patricia were here with him. They were very smart.

Maybe he should run back home, or — wait! An idea! He would go see the friendly men and women who drove the cars and trucks with the sirens and the flashing lights! Yay! He had a plan!

Happily, the dog jumped up and dashed towards the fire station. It was only about a quarter of a mile away, and the police station was located in the building next door. He had been there many times with the Callahans when they stopped by to say hello to Uncle Steve. Uncle Steve would *absolutely* help him, and the other officers probably would, too. Lots of times, when he was involved in adventures around town, the men and women in uniforms would mysteriously show up to assist him at some point. They were very good helpers.

When he ran up to the public safety complex, one of the rescue ambulances was just returning to headquarters. There had been so many car accidents during the last few hours, that the firefighters and paramedics had been extremely busy. This ambulance was being driven by paramedic Fran Minelli, and her partner, Saul Rubin. They had had an exhausting shift so far, and were looking forward to having a few minutes to relax and sip some hot coffee before being called out again.

The dog waited until they had parked the ambulance, and then he barked an energetic, but respectful bark.

Fran saw him first, and tapped her partner's arm. "Better hold off on that cup of coffee, Saul."

Saul looked over, and then groaned. "So much for our break. Think there's any chance he's crying wolf?" He bit his lip thoughtfully. "Or — crying shepherd?"

"Not a chance in the world," Fran said.

Saul felt the same way, but he had been hoping that she would disagree with him. "What's up, Santa Paws?" he asked, sounding resigned.

The dog barked, ran towards the street, then ran back to them.

"Okay." Fran hauled an aid bag out of the ambulance. "I'll follow on foot in case it's right nearby, and you drive."

Saul nodded, and slid behind the wheel of the rescue vehicle.

Santa Paws was so fast that Fran soon realized she didn't have a hope of being able to keep up. She motioned for Saul to pull over, and then climbed into the passenger's seat. It seemed clear from the dog's urgent behavior that there was a *serious* emergency waiting for them somewhere.

Santa Paws led the ambulance efficiently to Mr. Spiegel's house. Then, once they had parked, he stepped aside to let them take over.

" 'Crying shepherd,' " Fran muttered to Saul, when they saw Mr. Spiegel lying in his driveway in obvious distress.

Saul shrugged defensively, and grabbed some supplies and a cardiac kit from the back of the ambulance.

"Hello, Mr. Spiegel," Fran said, as she bent over him to take his vital signs. "Don't worry, you're going to be just fine now."

Abigail poked her head out from inside Mr. Spiegel's coat, and Fran jumped in surprise.

"Oh, my," she said. "Is your cat friendly?"

"Yes, my cat is extremely friendly," Mr. Spiegel answered.

Fran reached down to lift Abigail out of the way. Annoyed by having been so rudely awakened, Abigail hissed at her and slashed a warning paw in her direction. Fran swiftly withdrew her hand.

"I, uh, thought your cat was friendly," she said.

"Well, yeah, *my* cat is," Mr. Spiegel told her.

Fran and Saul finally caught on to the joke, and they both laughed. *This wasn't his cat.* If Mr. Spiegel could kid around — and make a reference to a Pink Panther movie, no less — then his prognosis had to be pretty good.

Pleased by her power to intimidate, Abigail jumped off Mr. Spiegel and flounced over to the side of the driveway to wash her face.

"Did the cat just show up out of nowhere?" Saul asked curiously, as he did a quick EKG, glanced at the results, and rechecked Mr. Spiegel's vital signs. Fran was on her mobile unit, calling ahead to the hospital to let them know that they were about to be transporting a probable cardiac arrest victim.

Mr. Spiegel shrugged, although it was somewhat difficult for him to move with the small monitor and IV hooked up to him. "No idea. She showed up with Santa Paws."

Fran and Saul looked at each other.

"Strange," Saul said. "He's always been a loner."

Fran nodded. "Classic hero archetype."

Santa Paws waited a few feet away, until he was sure that everything was under control. Then he barked once, and headed towards the street. Afraid that she might be left behind, Abigail hustled after him.

"Thank you, Santa Paws!" Mr. Spiegel shouted weakly.

The dog wagged his tail and trotted away. Now that he had done his job, he could go back to looking for the Callahans!

At the house, Gregory and Patricia were trying to help their father deal with the tree in the middle of the living room. First they had carried all of the Christmas presents, and anything else that might be damaged by exposure to the elements, into the den for safekeeping. Now it was time to figure out what to do with the actual *tree*.

"Maybe we should just leave it there," Patricia suggested. "So there's, you know, evidence of wrongdoing."

"Actually, I think this falls more into the category of an 'act of God,' Patricia," Mr. Callahan said.

Gregory had been extremely upset when Mr. Callahan vetoed the idea of their going out into the storm to search for Santa Paws and the cats, so cleaning up the mess was a good way for him to take his mind off things. "Should I go get the camera?" he asked. "So you have like, a photographic record for the insurance company?"

Mr. Callahan considered that, and then nodded. "Yeah, actually. That's a very good idea."

They took pictures of the tree from every possible angle. Then Mr. Callahan began to snap off branches, with the idea of gradually breaking the tree into manageable pieces.

"This is going to take forever, Dad," Patricia said, after a while. "I think we need someone with a chainsaw." All they had accomplished so far was to create a large pile of branches on the floor — while the tree still seemed to be just as big as when they had started.

"Yeah, really," Gregory said. "Maybe we should just close the door and worry about it tomorrow. Besides, I'm kind of getting hungry."

Mr. Callahan looked at his watch, blinked, and took a second look.

"What?" Patricia asked uneasily.

"It's just later than I thought," Mr. Callahan said. "I wonder where your mother is."

"Christmas shopping," Gregory reminded him.

"I know," Mr. Callahan said, "but — "

Frowning, he walked over to the telephone to make sure that there was a dial tone. The lights were flickering or fading every so often, and the phones might be on the verge of going out, too. But the dial tone sounded normal.

He hung up, frowning harder. "I'm surprised she hasn't called to tell us to go ahead and start dinner without her, that's all."

Considering how badly things had been going today, Patricia got nervous. "You don't think there's anything wrong, do you? I mean, it *always* takes her forever when she goes Christmas shopping."

"Absolutely," Mr. Callahan said, his voice a shade too jovial to be entirely convincing. "Let's go make some supper, so it'll be ready by the time she gets here."

Quietly, Gregory and Patricia followed him out to the kitchen. They were sure that their mother was all right, but they were still concerned.

Where *was* she?

Mrs. Callahan was in trouble. The large tree had smashed into the station wagon, crushing the hood and badly cracking the windshield. To make matters worse, it had hit some power lines on its way down and knocked over a telephone pole, too. The telephone pole had landed on the back end of the station wagon, hemming her in.

The accident had happened so quickly that it left Mrs. Callahan stunned. The force of the crash had slammed her into the steering wheel, and while she wasn't quite unconscious, she wasn't exactly *alert*, either.

She wasn't sure how much time had passed before she tried to sit up. When she finally moved, there was such a sharp pain in her ribs that she gasped. She had been wearing her seatbelt, but the station wagon was so old that it didn't have air bags.

Slowly and cautiously, she eased herself back against the seat. It was painful, but she didn't feel any severe pain until she tried to take a deep breath. So, for lack of a better idea, she resolved not to take any more deep breaths.

The dashboard had collapsed from the weight of the tree, but Mrs. Callahan was able to pull her right leg free without any trouble. Her left leg seemed to be stuck — and to be broken. It was twisted at an odd angle, and it *definitely* hurt a great deal.

"This is not good," she found herself saying aloud.

The engine seemed to be releasing steam, but it was hard to tell through the thick sleet. She turned the ignition key experimentally, but nothing happened. Afraid suddenly that she was doing something dangerous, Mrs. Callahan turned the ignition off. She couldn't smell any gas leaking, but she didn't want to take any chances.

The windows were up, but it was already starting to get cold inside the car. The windshield was cracked in so many places that frigid air was leaking steadily inside. Since the windows were automatic and didn't have handles, they wouldn't work if the engine was dead. So while she might freeze to death, at least the damaged windshield meant that she wouldn't *suffocate*.

Trying to find a short-cut home had unquestionably been a mistake. On a normal night, with no storm, the police department might send a cruiser on a routine patrol through this part of town. But with the horrible weather, tonight they would be concentrating their efforts in the areas where people actually *lived*.

She could walk to a populated street without much trouble, if she hadn't injured her leg. She could also beep the horn endlessly, but who would hear it? If *only* she had had the good sense to buy a cellphone, long ago. But — she had never really needed one before. Putting off that particular purchase was a decision she certainly regretted now!

She couldn't think of a solution to this situation, so she closed her eyes and took several — shallow — breaths. Her leg was hurting so much that it was difficult to think clearly. But she knew how worried her family was going to be if she didn't get home soon, so she *had* to think of something sensible to do.

Taking a couple of ibuprofen would be a good start. Mrs. Callahan fumbled around in the darkness until she found her purse. Teaching all day sometimes gave her headaches, so she always carried a bottle of aspirin or some other pain reliever. She located the bottle and swallowed two of the pills. They tasted terrible dry, and she felt around inside the bag for something to get rid of the bitterness. There were a few cough drops floating around at the bottom, and she put one in her mouth. Neither of these actions were a solution, but they were better than just *sitting* here.

It was very cold. She was already wearing her gloves and a knitted hat, and now she buttoned her coat all the way up to her neck. Maybe, if she was lucky, instead of freezing, she might just get — chilly.

Maybe.

But, like Patricia, she was not a very patient person. Even though it would be horribly painful, she should probably just walk, or limp, her way to the nearest occupied house. It was really the best way to handle this.

"Okay, then," Mrs. Callahan said aloud, to give herself confidence.

Using both gloved hands, she tugged on her pinned leg. It hurt even more than she had expected it would, but to make matters worse, it also didn't *budge*. She reached down with her left hand to move the seat back, which set off such a strong jolt of pain in her leg that she was afraid she might faint. Having the seat further back gave her more room to maneuver, but her leg stayed at the same sickening angle. She had a sinking feeling that the only way she would be able to free herself was if she used a *blow-torch* on the dashboard and steering column.

Unfortunately, she did not have a blow-torch handy.

Maybe opening the driver's side door would help. She could turn more easily that way, and it might result in her leg slipping free. Even if it didn't work, it was certainly worth a try.

As Mrs. Callahan reached for the door handle, she became aware of a strange crackling sound, above and beyond the howling of the storm. She listened intently, noticing for the first time that there seemed to be tiny flashes of light around and near the car at unpredictable intervals. Not only that, but the light flashes were *blue*. Crackling and blue flashes meant only one thing.

She was surrounded by live wires!

10

Mr. Callahan fixed roast beef sandwiches for Gregory and Patricia's supper, but he didn't bother making one for himself.

"Aren't you hungry, Dad?" Gregory asked with his mouth full.

"Late lunch," Mr. Callahan said. He was looking out the window with a pensive expression, which was probably better than his staring at the telephone as though that would *make* it ring.

Gregory and Patricia wanted to tell him not to worry — but he might get mad, and besides, they were worried, too. So they ate their sandwiches without much conversation, and even voluntarily chose nutritious fresh apples for dessert, instead of ice cream or cookies. Evelyn had made an appearance halfway through the meal, meowing for her own dinner, and they were glad to discover that *one* of their pets was at home where she belonged. Abigail might be lurking somewhere, too, but they hadn't seen her yet.

"Um, you could call Uncle Steve, maybe," Patricia said.

Mr. Callahan turned away from his post at the window, in an attempt to make his concern less obvious. "No, I think they probably have their hands full over there. I'm sure she'll be here any minute now."

Many minutes had already passed, but Gregory and Patricia simply cleared the table and cleaned up the kitchen without arguing. Mr. Callahan was so distracted that he didn't even seem to notice any of this.

"Can I ask again if we can go look for Santa Paws?" Gregory whispered.

Patricia shook her head. "He's too upset, and he's *never* going to let us go outside," she whispered back.

Gregory knew she was right, so he stayed silent.

If anything, the storm seemed to be getting worse. The winds sounded as though they were reaching hurricane force, and there were regular loud cracks and snaps as tree branches gave way from the weight of the ice.

It was time for a television show they liked, but none of them was exactly in the mood to watch a situation comedy right now.

"Do either of you know *where* she was going to shop?" Mr. Callahan asked. "Was she just going to go downtown, or was she heading all the way out to the mall?" The center of Oceanport was small, but had a surprisingly wide variety of stores crammed together within the space of a few blocks. Some of the shops, like Mabel's Five and Dime, were notoriously well-stocked, with all sorts of fun and interesting potential gifts tucked away on tall wooden shelves.

Gregory and Patricia looked at each other, and shrugged.

"She was buying presents, Dad. If she told us which stores she was going to, we could guess what she was getting," Gregory said logically.

Mr. Callahan checked the clock one last time, and then went over to get his coat. "I'm going to take a quick ride over there, see if I run into her."

Gregory looked eager. "Can we come, too? And maybe look for Santa Paws along the way?"

"No," Mr. Callahan said. "You two stay here. No point in *all* of us being out there in that mess. If your mother gets back here before I do, just tell her where I went, and that I'll be home soon."

"Yeah, but if we came, we could — " Gregory started.

"*No*," Mr. Callahan said firmly. "Really. I won't be gone long. Please just stay put, okay?"

It probably wasn't necessary to point this out, but Patricia said it, anyway. "Drive carefully, Dad."

"*Extremely* carefully," Mr. Callahan said, and headed outside.

Once the door had closed behind him, Gregory and Patricia looked at each other.

"Now what?" Gregory asked.

"I don't know." Then, Patricia sighed. "We could go check our email, I guess."

That seemed like a reasonably good way to kill time, so Gregory nodded and they started upstairs.

It really wasn't that late yet, but they had had such an eventful day, that it already *felt* like the middle of the night!

Santa Paws and Abigail were down near Main Street. So far, they had not seen, heard, or smelled any sign of the Callahans. Abigail was cold and exhausted — and the dog was starting to run out of enthusiasm, too. It had been *hours* since he had eaten, and his supper was long overdue.

Most of the stores had closed early because of the storm, and the street was almost completely deserted. Every so often, a car would creep past them, with an anxious driver behind the wheel. Other than that, they were pretty much alone.

Out of the blue, Abigail abruptly sat down in front of Sally's Diner and Sundries Shop, and refused to move another step. The dog used his paw to try and force her to start walking again, but Abigail wouldn't budge an inch. She wanted to go home *right now*, and that was all there was to it!

The dog considered leaving her, but the truth was, he was tired of this endless search, too. And maybe the Callahans had come home by now! It would be worthwhile to go back and check.

The minute he turned to face in the direction that led back to the house, Abigail sprang to her feet. She was always pleased when the dog saw things *her* way. Luckily, he was very easy to manipulate.

They had only made it about fifty feet when the dog paused. Abigail smacked him indignantly across the muzzle, but Santa Paws didn't even flinch. He just spun around and ran back down Main Street.

Once again, duty called!

Less than twenty minutes after Mr. Callahan left the house, the power went out. The multiple windows on Patricia's computer screen blacked out in an instant, and the television show Gregory was watching disappeared right in the middle of a punch line. They each sat very still, waiting for the power magically to return. Naturally, it didn't, and so they got up to go find each other — and some flashlights.

They met on the landing at the bottom of the stairs. In fact, they banged into each other.

"Power's out," Gregory said.

Patricia gasped. "No. Really?"

Since it was pitch black, he knew she couldn't see him blushing. "Yeah, well, you're the oldest," he said. "What do we do?"

"Light a big bonfire in the middle of the den and dance around it," she said.

Gregory took a step backwards and slammed right into the wall. "Whoa. And — *ow*," he added. "That seems like a totally bad idea, Patty."

Patricia nobly overlooked that extraordinarily gullible response. "Dad left all those flashlights in the kitchen. Let's go get them."

They ended up sitting at the kitchen table, so that they would only have to use one of the flashlights and could conserve the batteries. Even with the beam of the light brightening the room a little, it still seemed almost oppressively dark — and kind of scary.

"I hope they get back soon," Gregory said.

"They will," Patricia reassured him. "Mom just lost track of time, I bet. And — the lines at the stores were probably really long." That was the answer they both wanted to hear, so that was the one she gave.

"Yeah, that makes sense." Gregory shifted in his chair restlessly. "How come the furnace went off? We don't have electric heat."

"No, but the motor needs electricity to run," Patricia said. "Or a generator or something."

"Oh." Gregory started to open the refrigerator to get something to eat, but then paused. "We should probably keep this closed, right? Until the power comes back on?"

"Yeah." Patricia stood up. "You know, maybe I'll give Rachel a call. This might be flipping her out."

"Why? How would she even know the lights went out?" Gregory asked curiously.

"She'll know that the heat stopped, and that her computer isn't working or anything," Patricia said. "Besides, her mother was going down to the city to pick up her father at the airport, so she's the only one home."

Gregory shrugged. "All the flights were probably canceled."

"Maybe," Patricia said, and dialed her friend's number. When no one answered after a dozen rings, she hung up. "I wonder if their phone's out. I mean, I *know* she's supposed to be home right now."

"Maybe they went somewhere," Gregory guessed.

Patricia shook her head. "In the middle of this? No way." Then she looked very thoughtful, nodded once to herself, and went to get her coat.

"What are you doing?" Gregory asked suspiciously.

"I'll just run over there and make sure everything's okay," Patricia said, pulling on her jacket.

"I'll be back before Mom and Dad even know I left."

Gregory frowned at her. "That's totally stupid."

"Yeah," Patricia agreed, "so?"

Gregory couldn't think of a good retort for that. "Well, then, I'm coming with you."

"No, you have to stay here in case they *do* get here first," Patricia said.

Gregory hated being put in the middle of things like that. "What do I tell them, that you just took off and I couldn't stop you? They're going to be really mad."

Patricia nodded. "Yeah, say I overpowered you and then made my escape."

"You're too *thin* to overpower me," Gregory said grimly.

Patricia grinned and sat down on the floor to lace on one of her pairs of hockey skates.

Gregory stared at her. "Are you nuts?"

"With all that ice out there, this'll be easier," she said, knotting her bootlaces together and slinging them around her neck. That way, if she needed to walk at some point, she could change out of her skates. "I can make much better time."

He kept staring.

"It's not like I'm using my good game skates," she said, in her own defense.

Since it was impossible to talk Patricia out of something once she had her mind made up,

Gregory didn't bother trying. "You might as well wear your helmet, too."

Patricia's eyes lit up. "Good idea!" She used the wall for support as she stood up, since linoleum was not exactly the ideal surface for skate blades.

"Mom's going to be mad if you scratch up the floor," Gregory warned her.

"I know, I'm being careful." Patricia stepped delicately over to the backdoor, and then eased herself out to the patio. She took a couple of experimental glides forward, and while the surface was uneven, it still worked pretty well. "See?" she said triumphantly. "I'll be back in about twenty minutes."

Watching her skate down the back walk and out to the street, Gregory came to the conclusion that while it *was* a dumb plan, it just might work. He went back inside, rehearsing exactly what he was going to say if his parents happened to arrive home first.

The one thing he knew for sure was that Patricia was really going to *owe* him one.

He sat in the kitchen for a while, eating graham crackers and reading *People* magazine by flashlight. Mysteries and horror books were his favorites, but he didn't want to read anything creepy while he was here alone, in the dark.

Then it crossed his mind that since he *was*

stuck here by himself, this was the perfect opportunity to go out and look for Santa Paws and — possibly — Abigail. If human beings weren't supposed to be wandering around in this storm, pets weren't, either. He could at least walk around the block and call them a few times. If his dog heard his voice, Gregory knew that he would come running right away.

So Gregory bundled up, wrote a note for his parents explaining where he and Patricia had gone, and left the house.

Call him crazy, but he had elected *not* to wear skates.

When Santa Paws had sensed danger on Main Street, he had run straight to Harold's Happy Hardware Store. Harold had closed up for the night two hours earlier and let his employees go home, but he had stayed in the back office to work on inventory paperwork. Since he could walk home from his store, he wasn't worried about driving through the sleet.

Abigail trudged after him, so tired that her paws kept slipping on the ice. They should have been halfway home by now, but, *no*. The dog was running off to someone's rescue again. With every step, she planned some fiendish ways to take her revenge. Once they were home, she was going to eat from the dog's dish — whenever she wanted, scratch him a few times when his back was turned, and meow *really* loudly in his ear when he was asleep.

Harold was locking the front door of his store and double-checking to be sure that everything was secure. He had considered nailing plywood across the front windows to protect them from the storm, but that was really more suitable for hurricanes. There was a creaking sound coming from somewhere, but when he looked around, he couldn't locate the source. So he shrugged and put his keys into his pocket.

Out of nowhere, a large dark shape came barreling out of the night towards him. It looked like some kind of wild and vicious animal! Harold screamed and threw his arms up to protect his face.

He was about to be attacked!

11

There was no time to waste, and Santa Paws launched himself powerfully into the air. There was a parked car in his way, so he vaulted right over it. He slammed into Harold at chest-level, using all of his strength to knock him down. Harold groaned as he landed flat on his back on the ice. When he recognized his silent assailant, he was shocked.

"Santa Paws, what on earth do you think you're doing?" he demanded angrily. "That really — "

Just then, the heavy metal sign above his store tore free from its supports and came crashing down onto the exact spot where Harold had just been standing. The sign probably weighed more than two hundred pounds, and it hit the ground with such force that it actually dented in several places.

"Oh," Harold said. "Never mind." If Santa

Paws hadn't come along at just the right moment, he would have been crushed!

The crisis was over, so Abigail meowed sulkily. It was time to *go home* already.

The dog instantly turned and loped over to her. Whenever possible, he liked to avoid letting cats get into snits. And — his work was done here.

"Thanks, Santa Paws!" Harold called after him. "I'm going to give your family permanent discounts!"

The dog barked in his direction, without pausing in his steady trot. Then he and the cat disappeared into the stormy night.

While Mr. Callahan drove out to the mall, he saw numerous cars that had slid off the road, crashed, or run into other forms of trouble. Each time, he slowed down to make sure that his wife's station wagon wasn't there.

Despite the Christmas rush, the mall had closed half an hour early on the advice of the Oceanport Police Department. The road conditions were just too hazardous for their customers and employees. By now, the parking lots were almost empty.

Mr. Callahan cruised through each of the lots, looking for their station wagon. It was nowhere in sight, so he stopped his car for a minute to decide what to do next.

Had she passed him on the way home? Quite possibly, they had just missed each other. With that cheering thought, Mr. Callahan began to look for a payphone. There were several near the main entrance of the mall, and he parked right in front.

When he dialed the house, the phone rang, and rang, and *rang*. His first instinct was to panic, but then he realized that the storm could easily have knocked their telephone service out. So, except for a brief spin through downtown Oceanport, he would go directly home.

With luck, the entire family — pets and all — would be there waiting for him!

Patricia was finding her skating strategy surprisingly successful. Every so often she would hit a rough patch, and take a spill. But, for the most part, it was smooth sailing all the way. With the power out, the streets seemed somewhat unfamiliar, and she had to be careful not to skate into fallen branches. More than once, she ran into a parked car, but she wasn't skating fast enough to get hurt.

The wind was so cold that it seemed to be whipping right inside her jacket, and the pounding sleet made it that much harder to see where she was going.

In the darkness, she almost glided right past Rachel's house. Fortunately, it had a distinctive wooden fence. Patricia used one of her skate blades to feel for the curb, and then stepped onto the sidewalk. She skated up to Rachel's front steps, and carefully made her way up the stairs. The house was completely dark, but Rachel wouldn't have had any reason to turn on a flashlight or light a candle.

Patricia took one of her gloves off and rapped loudly on the door with her bare hand. With the storm, the sound would be muffled, but Rachel had better hearing than anyone she knew. She let about a minute go by, and then knocked again.

"Hey, Rachel!" she yelled. "Open the door, okay?"

Once she was sure that no one was there, Patricia side-stepped down the stairs to the front walk. Either Rachel and her parents had gone somewhere, or Rachel was staying at a neighbor's house, waiting for her parents to come home. Patricia knew that Rachel's favorite neighbor was Mrs. Kravitz, who lived around the corner. If Rachel had gone *anywhere* by herself, that was the direction she would have taken. So it wouldn't hurt to go knock on Mrs. Kravitz's door, and see if her friend was there.

Patricia was at the end of the street, making a sharp right turn on her skates, when she heard something — or some*one* — moving along the sidewalk.

"Hello?" she said tentatively.

There was a pause, interrupted only by the howling whistle of the winds.

"Patricia?" a voice answered, sounding just as uncertain. "Is that you?"

Rachel! Patricia skated towards the voice, feeling very relieved. For one thing, she was pleased to have located her friend; for another, she was even *more* pleased that the person lurking nearby hadn't been an odious criminal or something. "Yeah. Are you going down to Mrs. Kravitz's?"

"I *was*," Rachel admitted. "But — well, I kind of got turned around. There's like, all these branches and stuff on the ground, and — everything's *different*. I'm not really sure where my house is." Since she didn't have a guide dog yet, Rachel had to depend on nothing more than her cane — and her memory — when she wanted to go somewhere. Whenever the desks got rearranged at school, or anyone she knew redecorated their house, it was a real challenge for Rachel to get around until she memorized the new layout.

"It *is* different," Patricia said. "I've been pretty disoriented, too."

"Why do your shoes sound weird?" Rachel asked.

Patricia grinned. "Because they're hockey skates."

"Figures," Rachel said, and laughed. "How'd

you know I'd be dumb enough to be walking around in the middle of all this?"

Patricia shrugged. "Takes one to know one."

"That's for sure. I'm really glad they did, but I can't *believe* your parents let you come over here," Rachel said.

Thinking about how they would react if her parents got home before she did, Patricia felt guilty. "They didn't. My mother's late coming back from shopping, and my father went to look for her, so I — snuck out."

"Looks like *you'll* be grounded for the rest of vacation," Rachel said wryly. "But, then again, *I* probably will be, too."

Once they had established that Rachel's parents hadn't come home yet either, Patricia sat down on the curb to change into her boots. Then Patricia guided her back to her house so that she could leave a note saying that she was at the Callahans.

"I've been out there for a pretty long time," Rachel confessed. "I could have gone up to a house, but I was too embarrassed to tell whoever answered the door that I was lost. I figured I'd find my way home eventually."

Patricia laughed. "Well, I guess when it comes to the Seven Deadly Sins, you've got *pride* nailed."

"It's better than greed or gluttony," Rachel said.

"Yeah," Patricia agreed, "but sloth kind of appeals to me."

Once they were back outdoors, they picked their way carefully across the ice. They were making good progress until a ferocious blast of wind tore some already sagging power lines down right in front of them.

"What?" Rachel asked, when Patricia stopped.

"A bunch of telephone wires and stuff just came down," Patricia said. "You think it's safe to go by them because the power's out?"

"No way," Rachel said instantly. "They could still be charged somehow."

Since it wasn't worth risking their lives to find out — it was important to avoid *any* downed power line, no matter what — they went a couple of blocks out of their way, instead. That put them right by Patricia's aunt and uncle's darkened house. Since Aunt Emily had a cellular telephone, it seemed like a good idea for them to go in and have Patricia make a quick call home — just in case.

When Aunt Emily opened the door, Miranda was yelling and bouncing around in the background. There was a small camp lantern giving off an orange glow in the living room. Aunt Emily looked tense and exhausted — and surprised to see them.

"What are you two doing out on a night like this?" she asked. "Come on in." She looked at Patricia's helmet curiously. "Nice hat, Patricia."

"Patty, Patty, Patty!" Miranda shouted exuberantly. "Merry Christmas! Did you bring me any presents? And tomorrow is my birthday, too!" She smiled widely at Rachel. "I'm going to be a big girl."

Miranda had been saying "Merry Christmas" to everyone she met for about three months now. "Merry Christmas, Miranda. We're really sorry to just show up, Aunt Emily," Patricia said, "but I think I need to call home and let my parents know where I am. Could I use your cell phone?"

Aunt Emily shook her head. "I'm sorry, the battery's dead. I was just going to recharge it when the power went out." She rubbed one hand wearily across the back of her neck. "I'm afraid that the regular telephone isn't working, either."

Patricia was about to apologize again for their showing up unannounced, and say that they would just head home, when she noticed how gingerly her aunt was moving across the room. "Is everything okay?"

Aunt Emily waved that aside, as she lowered herself onto the couch. "Just some minor contractions, no big deal."

Contractions certainly *sounded* like a big deal. "Um, but you still have two months left," Patricia said.

Aunt Emily nodded. "I know. It's probably just

false labor. So Miranda and I have been trying to keep quiet, right, Miranda?"

"Yes!" Miranda said, as she pounded away on her tiny piano keyboard. "I am a *very* good girl."

"Don't mind me, girls, if I just lie down here for a minute," Aunt Emily said. She stretched out on the couch, resting her legs up on two pillows.

"Does Uncle Steve know?" Patricia asked.

Aunt Emily shook her head. "No, it started after the phones stopped working. He's supposed to be off at midnight, but I'm guessing he'll have to pull a double-shift tonight."

"But you'd rather he knew about it," Patricia said.

Aunt Emily hesitated. "Well — I mean — "

"Got it," Patricia said, and sat down on the floor to put on her skates.

It looked as though a quick trip down to the police station was in her immediate future.

The sleet was coming down so hard that Gregory made a point of staying within a block or two of his house. He wanted to find Santa Paws and Abigail, but that didn't mean he had to be *stupid* about it. He had brought along a flashlight, so that it would be easier to see where he was going — and if there was anything dangerous in his way.

The storm was probably drowning out the sound of his voice, but he kept calling out, "Santa Paws! Come here, Santa Paws!" Every so often, he threw in a shout for Abigail, too, even though he knew that she went out of her way *not* to answer to her name. But the click of a catfood can — or any can, really — opening could wake her up from the deepest sleep in about a second and a half.

The sleet seemed to be freezing onto his jacket and hat, and Gregory wondered if this was just a waste of time. He was starting to get *really* cold. Besides, Santa Paws had found his way home before, and he would have no trouble doing it again. But that didn't mean that Gregory wasn't worried about him.

"Santa Paws!" he yelled. "Come here, boy!"

To his delight, he heard a faint, and very familiar, answering bark! He stayed right where he was, aiming the flashlight beam down the murky street. It was hard to see through the sleet, and he held one hand above his eyes to try and sharpen his vision.

Santa Paws kept barking, and after another minute, he came galloping towards Gregory at top speed. He jumped on Gregory so joyfully that they both tumbled onto the ice. But they were so glad to have found each other, that neither of them minded.

"Oh, good boy, you're very smart," Gregory said. "Let's go get some Milk-Bones."

The dog barked and wagged his tail energetically. A Milk-Bone would be fine, but it was more important that he had found his family! Part of his family, anyway. He was so happy! To celebrate, he leaped on Gregory again, and they both fell over a second time.

Gregory was just getting up when a small black shape streaked towards him and sprang right into his arms.

"Well, hi, Abigail," Gregory said, and patted her with his frozen glove. "What a pretty girl."

Abigail liked being called pretty, and she started purring. From her perspective, it was all well and good that she had found Gregory, but better than that, now she would get to be carried home!

Mrs. Callahan was still trapped in her car. It was incredibly frustrating not to be able to go for help, but with the wires snapping and crackling in the wind, she was frankly afraid to *move*. Staying in the car was the safest choice. Of course, with her leg pinned, it was really her *only* choice.

It was so cold that her teeth had started chattering. For some reason, she also felt terribly sleepy and kept dozing off. The pain from her injuries was pretty intense, but she was still having trouble staying awake. She was not what you would call an outdoors person, but she knew enough to realize that falling asleep in freezing temperatures was the worst possible thing to do. A lot of people who did that never woke up again.

She turned the key backwards in the ignition to see if she could get the radio to work. Unfortunately, the electrical system seemed to be dead along with everything else, because nothing happened when she turned the dial. Her hazard lights also wouldn't go on. That would have made it much easier for someone else to see her, but the weight of the tree must have crushed the engine almost completely.

The evening newspaper was on the front seat, and she tucked a couple of sections inside her coat for extra insulation. She also moved her arms and good leg to help get her blood flowing.

Staying warm — and awake — might be a matter of life or death!

12

Using one of Aunt Emily's flashlights to guide her path, Patricia was able to skate quite quickly. The surface was still rough and unforgiving, but she was nothing if not an aggressive athlete. She glided up to the public safety complex just as Fran and Saul were returning from taking Mr. Spiegel, the heart attack victim, to the Emergency Room. The doctors on duty had said that Santa Paws had gone for help just in time, and that Mr. Spiegel would make a full recovery.

Saul recognized Patricia and waved cheerily. "Hi, are you looking for your dog? You just missed him."

"Really?" Patricia said. "What was he doing?"

Fran unloaded the kit they had used from the back of the ambulance, so that they could restock the supplies. "Rescuing a cardiac case along with some cat. Kind of a *mean* cat."

That wasn't the answer Patricia had expected

to hear, but it was good to know that Abigail was safe, and up to her usual tricks. And if Santa Paws had completed his rescue, they were probably on their way home now.

"Well — that's good," she said. "Good for them. Um, I think *I* might need your ambulance, too."

Tired as they were, Saul and Fran snapped to attention.

"Not for me," Patricia assured them. "My aunt is having some contractions, and she isn't sure if it's, you know, Braxton Hicks" — which was a form of false labor — "or if she should go to the hospital."

"You're right, we'd better get over there." Fran turned towards a patrol officer just heading out of the station to get into his squad car. "Hey, Timmy! Is Steve Callahan around anywhere? His wife's having some premature contractions."

"Let me raise him on the radio," Timmy responded. "I think he's out at that big accident on Fairfax. Should he go home, or meet you at the hospital?"

"Patch him through on our frequency," Saul said. "We'll update him once we know more." He motioned Patricia over. "Come on, you'll ride with us."

Patricia skated to the passenger's side door, noticing that her skates blades were starting to get *very* dull and unresponsive. They might not

have been exposed to ideal conditions tonight —
but they had really come in handy when she
needed them!

The paramedics drove her back to Aunt
Emily's house. Earlier that evening, they had
paused to put chains on their tires, so the ambulance handled the roads with very little skidding. Aunt Emily wasn't eager to go to the
hospital, but after talking to Uncle Steve over
the handheld radio, she agreed.

In the meantime, a squad car arrived to take
Patricia, Rachel — and Miranda — to Patricia's
house. The police officers were pleased to see
Rachel, because her mother had just gotten in
touch with the Oceanport station house from
Boston, to say that she was stuck in the city because of the weather, and could they please send
someone over to check on her daughter and see
if she needed anything. Apparently, Rachel's father's flight had been grounded in Baltimore, so
he wouldn't be home anytime soon, either.

To keep Aunt Emily from worrying, Patricia
went upstairs to pack a few of Miranda's favorite
stuffed animals, her pink "grown-up lady" purse,
and a Little Mermaid nightgown. It looked as
though the Callahans would be doing some unexpected babysitting tonight!

When Mr. Callahan drove up his street, he was
alarmed to see a police car stopping in front of

141

his house. He jumped out of the Buick almost before he had a chance to turn off the engine.

"What's going on?" he asked nervously.

Patricia was holding Miranda's hand to help her out of the car. Her cousin was a little confused by all of the activity. It was also past her bedtime and she had yawned the whole way over. "Hi, Dad," she said. "We're just — " She wasn't sure where to begin. "Miranda and Rachel are spending the night. It's kind of a long story."

Rachel knew the Callahans' house very well, so she had no trouble finding her way across the driveway to the back gate. She lifted her cane in a little wave. "Hi, Mr. Callahan. Thank you for having me over."

Hearing all of the commotion, Santa Paws started barking inside the house. Gregory peeked out the window, saw the cars, and went out to see what was happening.

"Merry Christmas, Gregory!" Miranda shouted.

"You, too, Miranda," he said, looking a little confused. "Hi, Rachel."

Rachel waved her cane in his direction this time.

"Well, if you're all set here," Officer Bronkowski said, "we'd better get back on patrol."

While everyone else was thanking Officer Bronkowski and her partner, Officer Lee, for their help, Gregory was looking around for the station wagon.

"Um, Dad?" he asked. "Where's Mom?"

When Mr. Callahan realized that his wife *hadn't* returned while he was gone, his face went completely pale.

"You kids go inside now, okay?" he said, once he was sure he could keep his voice reasonably steady. "Make sure Miranda's nice and warm. She could get a chill, being out in this."

Gregory and Patricia caught on at the exact same time, and they exchanged scared looks.

"Go on," their father insisted. "We'll talk in a few minutes."

Gregory and Patricia looked at each other again, and then Gregory reached for Miranda's free hand to help lead her across the ice. Rachel came along right behind them, just as quiet and uneasy as they were. Only Miranda was still chirping away about Christmas and her birthday, what fun it would be to play with the cats, and when would her mommy come to get her.

Once Mr. Callahan was sure they were out of earshot, he turned to Officers Bronkowski and Lee.

"I'm afraid we need you two to stick around for a few minutes and take a report," he said quietly. "It looks as though my wife is missing."

* * *

Once they were inside the house, Patricia busied herself with taking off Miranda's coat, hat, and mittens, while Gregory went to get her a cookie. Rachel sat down at the kitchen table, absent-mindedly patting Santa Paws.

"It's dark," Miranda said, sounding as though she was close to tears. "I don't like it. I want to go home."

"Okay, but first we're going to have fun here playing games," Patricia said. "So don't cry, Miranda."

Gregory held out the cookie. "You *can't* be sad when there are chocolate chips in the room."

Miranda's face brightened, and she took the snack from him. "Can we go play with Abigail?" she asked.

"Well, we can try," Gregory said doubtfully. Abigail was on the unpredictable side, as far as her moods were concerned. He lifted a small flashlight from the table and handed it to her. "Let's go look for her."

"Yay!" Miranda said, and directed the beam crazily around the room.

Rachel was sure she had already guessed what was going on, but once Gregory and Miranda were gone, she still had to ask. "When was your mother supposed to be home?"

"*Hours* ago," Patricia said, suddenly close to tears herself.

"She could just have a flat tire," Rachel said. "It doesn't have to be anything *bad*."

Patricia nodded. "I know." Her mother could also have tried to call and not been able to get through, or leave a message on the answering machine. But Patricia had a terrible feeling that something *awful* must have happened. Otherwise, her mother would have found a way to get home already.

When Mr. Callahan came in, it was obvious that he was so worried that he couldn't quite think straight. He sat down across from Patricia and Rachel, then brought both hands up to rub his forehead.

"Dad — " Patricia started.

"When did the power go out?" he asked.

"Right after you left," Patricia said.

Mr. Callahan nodded, and sucked in a deep breath, his hands still covering his eyes. Then he exhaled heavily and lowered his hands. "Okay," he said. "They're starting an official search. Can you three handle Miranda while I go and help them?"

"Of course," Patricia said, while Rachel was saying, "No problem, Mr. Callahan."

"Okay, good." He shook his head as though he'd lost his train of thought. "Bring all the sleeping bags to the den — that'll be the warmest room for now. You all can camp out in there.

And please don't light any candles. I'm afraid Miranda — or Santa Paws — might knock one over by accident. Just stick to the flashlights, we have plenty of batteries."

Hearing his name, the dog came over and rested his head on Mr. Callahan's knee. He could always tell when his family was upset, but he almost never knew *why*. His stomach was rumbling, and he wished that Mrs. Callahan would come home and give him his supper.

"Any questions?" he asked, giving Santa Paws a light pat.

Patricia had lots of questions, but all of them involved her mother, so she just shook her head.

"Okay." Mr. Callahan stood up. "In case I can't get back here right away, I'll make sure Steve has a car sent by to check on you every so often. Just sit tight, and — " His voice broke. "And, um, I'm sure everything's going to be all right."

There wasn't much else to say, so Patricia just hugged him and stuck an apple in his coat pocket in case he got hungry later. Then, as he plunged into the storm, she looked at Rachel.

"Guess we'd better go get those sleeping bags," she said.

Rachel nodded, and they headed upstairs to the attic.

It was way past her bedtime, but Miranda had no interest in going to sleep. Abigail had made it very clear that she did not want to play, so Miranda settled for throwing a tennis ball for Santa Paws to fetch. The dog was happy to cooperate, no matter how wildly she threw the ball. Patricia finally bribed her into a sleeping bag, by promising that they would use a flashlight to make shadow puppets on the wall for her.

At one point, Police Officers Littlejohn and Nichols knocked on the back door. They had no news about Mrs. Callahan yet, but they reported that Aunt Emily was feeling better, and had been admitted for overnight observation as a precaution. The only thing they knew about the search was that it was "ongoing."

Gregory thanked them and returned to the den. He shook his head in answer to Patricia's unasked question. Patricia's face fell, but she nodded.

She handed him a pair of scissors and some construction paper. "Here. Miranda wants you to make Santa Claus and *all* of his reindeer."

Gregory's mouth dropped open. "What?" The only shadow puppets he could really manage were simple things like rabbits, and cats.

"Don't forget Rudolph," Patricia said. "Go to it."

Gregory gritted his teeth and started cutting the paper.

After what felt like an infinite number of shadow puppets, Miranda finally fell asleep. Patricia and Rachel were also having a hard time staying awake, although they were trying their best.

The dog came over to nudge Gregory's leg, and Gregory knew he needed to go outside. That gave him an idea and he walked softly out of the room, being careful not to disturb anyone. He put on his still-damp jacket, and then took a sweatshirt of his mother's out of the laundry basket in the pantry.

"I want you to find Mom," he whispered, and then held the sweatshirt out for Santa Paws to smell. "Okay? *Find Mom.*"

The dog obediently sniffed the sweatshirt, and cocked his head to one side. What did Gregory want? Didn't he know that that was Mrs. Callahan's shirt? What was he supposed to find?

Gregory tucked the sweatshirt into his jacket and scrawled a fast note, in case Patricia woke up. It read: "Took the dog out. Back soon." Then he put on Santa Paws' leash, found a dry pair of gloves, and slipped outside.

The temperature had dropped enough so that the freezing rain was more like hard snow now. It was well below freezing, but the light covering of granular snow made it easier to walk without slipping. Once they were in the driveway, Gregory held the sweatshirt out again.

"Concentrate, Santa Paws," he said. "I want you to *find Mom.*"

The dog sniffed the sweatshirt, and held his paw up uncertainly.

"Find Mom," Gregory said. "Find the car."

The dog knew all of those words, but following cars was so hard! He had already tried — and failed — to do that once tonight.

Gregory also wasn't sure where to start. There were so many different ways to drive home from the mall, and his mother could have taken any one of them. That is, if she had *gone* to the mall in the first place. She could have done her shopping down near Main Street, or in one of the neighboring towns, or — there were too many possibilities. But he had to make a guess, and the mall seemed to be her most likely choice. All he could do was start leading Santa Paws in that general direction, and then just hope that they got lucky.

"Good boy," he kept saying, to encourage him. "Find Mom. *Fetch* Mom."

The dog walked steadily forward, tilting his nose in the air, and then running it along the snow in a regular pattern. If there was a scent *anywhere*, somehow he would locate it.

They were covering more ground than Gregory had expected, and he wondered if it might be time to turn around. If he was gone too long, Patricia might wake up and get really upset. But as long as there was a chance that Santa Paws could find his mother, how could he not try?

No matter what he did, the dog couldn't seem to pick up a scent. It was upsetting not to be able to do what Gregory had asked, and he whined a few times.

"It's okay, you're good," Gregory said, hoping to console him. Maybe he shouldn't put so much pressure on his dog, especially when they were both so tired after such an incredibly grueling day. It might be better if he just left this up to the police.

Santa Paws kept forging ahead. If his nose wouldn't help him, he would have to rely on his instincts, instead. And his instincts were telling him to keep going forward. They also seemed to be pulling him — west. He was focusing so hard on the task at hand that he almost forgot that Gregory was at the other end of his leash. And he didn't even *notice* the thick layer of snow starting to coat his fur.

Gregory had no idea where they were going, but trusting Santa Paws had never once been the wrong choice. His dog seemed so preoccupied that Gregory just trailed after him without another word, not wanting to interfere in any way. He was caught off-guard when Santa Paws halted, and it took a fancy bit of coordination to keep from falling right over him.

"What is it, boy?" he asked.

Santa Paws stood very still, concentrating intently. For a second, he thought he might have caught the tiniest whiff of — wait, there it was again! The dog turned his head to catch the wind just right, and try to confirm what he already sensed. Yes, the scent was distinct now.

He knew where Mrs. Callahan was!

13

Gregory understood his dog well enough to recognize the moment when he finally honed in on a scent. And Santa Paws had unquestionably tracked something down!

"Good boy," he said, trying to hold back his own excitement. "Find Mom!"

That was all the coaxing Santa Paws needed, and he bolted forward in the direction of the smell. Gregory tried to hang on to the leash, but Santa Paws wrenched it right out of his hands. The dog was so eager to follow the trail that he was a block away before he realized that he had left Gregory behind. He waited impatiently for Gregory to catch up.

"Slow down a little, okay?" Gregory said, breathing hard.

He retrieved the end of the leash, and Santa Paws set a more manageable, but still very rapid, pace. The dog was taking him towards a part of town where nobody lived, which seemed weird, but Gregory wasn't about to contradict him.

There was lots of debris, mainly branches, lying all over the ground. The flashlight helped a little, but the beam was too weak to light more than a short, narrow path. Santa Paws took several turns, leading him down curved, icy streets. There was plenty of construction going on around here, and Gregory could see the skeletons of houses silhouetted dimly against the sky. Someday, this would be a really nice suburban neighborhood, but right now, it just felt abandoned and creepy.

Further up ahead, Gregory thought he could make out the outline of a huge tree lying across the road. As they got closer, he saw that it *was* a tree, and it seemed to be lying on top of a car. A station wagon!

"Hey, Mom!" he yelled. "Are you in there?"

He dropped the leash and started running as fast as he could, terrified of what he might find. Then, when he was about sixty feet away, Santa Paws came racing over and slammed into his legs. Gregory lost his balance and fell painfully onto the ice and gritty snow.

Gregory shook his head, dazed by the unexpected spill. "Santa Paws, don't do that! You're right in the way."

To his complete astonishment, Santa Paws *growled* at him when he tried to get up. Then the dog stepped on his chest, pushing him back down. At first, Gregory's feelings were hurt, but then he was just angry.

"*No*," he said. "Bad dog!"

The dog's tail went between his legs, but he kept growling whenever Gregory made an attempt to move forward.

"Okay, okay," Gregory said, and cautiously slid back a few feet. That didn't earn him a growl, so he edged a little further away.

The dog seemed calmer now, but still looked wary.

Gregory took his time standing up, still stunned by what had just happened. Santa Paws was the most gentle dog in the world! Had the stress of the storm made him *completely* lose his mind?

The dog came over now, his head lowered in apology, and wagging his tail. Gregory patted him hesitantly, and the dog leaned against him, his tail whipping back and forth. Since everything seemed okay now, Gregory lifted his leg to take a tentative step. Santa Paws pressed firmly against his legs and forced him backwards.

"Okay, okay," Gregory said. He understood that his dog was trying to tell him something — and to *help* him, not hurt him. "You're a good boy."

Santa Paws wagged his tail in relief. He hated frightening Gregory, but how else could he warn him? The stench of burnt electricity was so strong that he couldn't figure out why Gregory didn't smell it, too.

"Take me to Mom," Gregory said. "Okay? Find Mom."

The dog whined softly. He didn't want to go near the car. The car was *bad*.

"Come on, Santa Paws," Gregory said, while he wrapped the end of the leash tightly around his hand and wrist. "Take me to the car."

The dog had to think. What should he do? Finally, he veered to the right and herded Gregory off the road and into the woods. He kept his body between Gregory and the bad car every step of the way. He led Gregory through the trees in a wide detour, so that they could approach the car from the other side. He brought him to within about forty feet of the car and then stopped, keeping them both well off the road.

Gregory gulped, and then flashed his light at the station wagon. He could see a figure slumped in the front seat, and he instinctively lunged towards the car. Santa Paws blocked his way firmly, and kept him right where he was.

Mom!" Gregory shouted at the top of his lungs. "Mom, are you okay?"

The figure stirred and looked groggily in his direction. In the thin beam of light, he could see that it was his mother — and she was alive!

"Mom, it's me!" Gregory said.

Mrs. Callahan was half-asleep, and she felt tired and confused. She thought she had heard her son's voice, but she must be hallucinating. However, the light shining at her face convinced her, and now she was wide awake. Her power window still wouldn't open, but she pried her fingers underneath the rubber guard and forced it down a couple of inches with more strength than she knew she had.

"Gregory, stay where you are!" she ordered through the crack. "Don't come anywhere near the car!"

"Why? I don't —" He thought he saw a bright blue light flicker, and he pointed the flashlight at the top of the car. "Oh, wow." Those were *live* power lines. No wonder Santa Paws had snarled at him! They could have been electrocuted!

"Where's your father?" Mrs. Callahan asked.

"With the police, looking for you," Gregory said. "I'm just here with Santa Paws. Are you okay?"

"I'm fine," Mrs. Callahan said briskly. "Make sure you don't come any closer. Can you go over to Sycamore —" which was a few streets away — "and call for help? There's a payphone at that convenience store."

Gregory had a better idea, especially since he didn't want to leave his mother alone. There was also a good chance that the phones were out on Sycamore Street, and the power might be, too.

He bent down and put his hands on either side of his dog's face.

"Santa Paws, *go find help*, okay?" he said. "We need *help*."

Help! Finally, an easy one! He knew how to find *that*. The dog barked, and then sprinted away into the darkness.

"He can go ten times faster than I can, Mom, but do you want me to start walking?" Gregory asked. "Or — is there something I can do to help? Like, keep you company, maybe?"

On the one hand, Mrs. Callahan didn't want Gregory within a *mile* of these wires. On the other hand, there could be other wires down elsewhere, and it wouldn't be safe for her son to be walking around without Santa Paws to protect him.

"Okay," Mrs. Callahan said finally. "But please don't move from where you are, no matter what."

Gregory nodded, although if the wind blew one of those wires in his direction, he would probably run like crazy. Even from here, he could see that his mother was shivering, and that worried him. She had been trapped in that car for hours now! "Are you sure you're all right, Mom?"

"Well, I may spend Christmas on crutches," she answered casually. "But let's talk about something else, okay?"

Crutches! "Um, sure," Gregory said. "Definitely."

This was followed by a long silence, since they were both tired, upset, and not thinking very clearly at this point.

"So," Gregory said, finally. "Nice weather we're having."

His mother's laugh sounded genuine, which made him feel much better.

"You're right," she said. "Couldn't be nicer."

It was quiet again.

"We trust Santa Paws implicitly, don't we?" Mrs. Callahan asked.

"Totally," Gregory said.

The dog knew that he couldn't maintain a full sprint all the way to the building where he had gone to see the nice, uniformed men and women earlier that night. It was *far*! So he settled into a smooth, steady lope. That way, he could cover a great deal of ground without having to stop and rest.

He had to slow down once, at an intersection, when a big, heavy truck rumbled past him. It was leaving a dense trail of small white crystals behind. When Santa Paws crossed the street, the crystals made his paws sting. He remembered that feeling from other winters. It was salt! Yuck!

He had to limp a little from the burning pain, before he resumed his regular gait. He was glad he only saw one or two cars, because it was much easier to run in the middle of the road. Having to dodge traffic always made rescues much more difficult. And this was *Mrs. Callahan* he was trying to help!

The thought of Gregory and Mrs. Callahan back on that cold, lonely road waiting for him gave the dog a burst of extra adrenaline. He picked up speed, bounding over drifts of snow, and branches lying in front of him. He dashed around one final corner and ran up to the fire station. The public safety complex was equipped with generators, so their power was still on at a reduced level.

There was no one in sight, and Santa Paws barked urgently at the main entrance. Everyone on duty, except for the dispatcher, was out tending to one emergency or another — or helping search for Mrs. Callahan. Santa Paws barked his very loudest bark, hoping that someone would hear him.

He stood up on his hind legs to paw at the door, and it opened! Whoever had left last hadn't closed it completely. The dog ran into the police station, barking frantically. The dispatcher, Eric Martinez, was busy coordinating all of Ocean-port's emergency service workers simultaneously. The near-hysterical barking was bothering him, and he looked up from his combination switchboard and radio relay system. When he saw a panting and snow-covered Santa Paws, he grabbed his receiver to make a system-wide announcement.

"All units, this is Dispatch," he said. "We have a probable canine 10-13 emergency here. Be advised that Santa Paws has just arrived at my location. Unit Ocean-Charles-Niner, are you available to respond?"

The squad car in question answered with an official 10-1, that they were now en route to quarters, with an ETA of approximately six minutes.

"Is Unit Ocean-Charles-Two still out of service?" Eric asked. Ocean-Charles-Two was Uncle Steve, although when he worked earlier shifts, he was either Ocean-Adam-Two, or Ocean-Bravo-Two. After receiving confirmation of that, Eric quickly switched gears to handle a call from another unit about a 10-40, Code 2, which was a car accident with a nonserious classification.

Santa Paws whined nervously, not sure why the man was talking on the telephone, instead of coming over to help him. He moved indecisively towards the exit, hesitated, and came back.

"All personnel should be aware that the male canine is in a highly agitated state at this time,"

Eric reported. "The subject's owner may want to 10-6 — " which was "stand-by" — "for possible assistance."

Santa Paws barked in an attempt to get his attention. Eric motioned for him to come over, and then patted him.

"Good dog," he said, covering the receiver with one hand. "They're on the way."

The dog didn't relax until he heard sirens outside. Yes! Help was here! He raced to the door, barking the whole way.

Officers Hank Littlejohn and Tracy Nichols were Unit Ocean-Charles-Niner.

"I hope those kids are all right," Hank said to his partner. "We should have been checking on them more often."

"We've been checking on the whole *town*," Tracy pointed out.

The dog barked at them, ran to the door where the ambulances usually were, barked again, ran to the street, and barked a third time.

Hank sighed. "It would be so much easier if someone could teach him how to talk."

Tracy watched intently as Santa Paws performed the exact same ritual again. "He's trying to tell us that this is big," she said. "That he needs more than one unit."

Hank was skeptical. He had always preferred cats to dogs. To his way of thinking, cats were *sensible.* "Does he mean he needs a fire truck or an ambulance?"

"How should I know?" Tracy asked. "I'm only making an educated guess."

Hank picked up the radio and requested immediate backup, including a "bus" — or ambulance — for the previously broadcast 10-13. The nearest rescue vehicle was the unit being driven by Saul and Fran. Only a couple of minutes passed before they pulled up in front of the station.

"Looks like you're having a hectic night, too," Saul said to Santa Paws.

Yay! People he knew would help him! The dog barked, ran out to the street, and waited for them to follow him.

Since Fran and Saul were already comfortable with the technique of following Santa Paws to an emergency scene, they went first. Hank and Tracy rode behind them, driving their squad car slowly.

The dog was pretty worn out by now, and he lost his footing a couple of times. Fran was so worried that she might hit him by accident, that she finally stopped the ambulance.

"He's had it," she said. "Either one of us needs to walk with him, or we should put him in here, and see if that works."

Since the dog *did* seem exhausted, Saul opened his door and whistled for him. The dog looked back over his shoulder wearily, but kept trotting forward.

"Come here, boy!" Saul called out. "We're going to try an experiment."

The dog loved to go for rides, but this did not seem like a good time. What did they want? Didn't they know that they had to hurry?

"Come on," Saul insisted.

Reluctantly, the dog obeyed. Saul patted the front seat, so that Santa Paws would know to jump inside. Then he climbed in after him and shut the door.

"Okay," he said. "Now what?"

Fran shrugged. "Trial and error, I guess. Whenever I miss a turn my dog expects me to take, she gets really upset. Maybe he'll do the same thing."

"Worth a try," Saul said.

Santa Paws wasn't very happy about being in the ambulance, and he squirmed around uncomfortably. But he stayed quiet as the ambulance continued up the street. Only then it went too far! They were going the wrong way! Help! He jumped up and started barking.

Fran had already radioed the squad car about what she was doing, so Hank and Tracy weren't surprised when she backed up and turned onto the street she had just gone by.

Yes! This was right! Santa Paws relaxed against the seat. But now it was time for another turn! What if they went past it? That would be bad! He got up and barked again, in anticipation of the intersection ahead of them.

Fran did her best to read that cue, and started to turn right.

Oh, no! This was wrong! What was she *doing*? Santa Paws kept barking, hoping that he could make her understand.

Fran stopped, backed up, and turned left this time.

Yes! That was good! The dog slouched back against the seat to rest for a minute. This was *so* stressful.

Slowly, but surely, he managed to guide them back to the street where Gregory and Mrs. Callahan were. This required a lot of barking, and a few episodes of flinging himself onto the seat in despair.

Since his view wasn't blocked by a huge tree, Gregory saw the flashing lights first.

"Mom, here they come," he said happily. "He did it!"

Once again, Santa Paws had saved the day!

14

Soon, more emergency vehicles arrived, followed by some workers from the local electric company. They were the only ones who knew how to shut down the power and remove the wires safely. Even the police and firefighters weren't trained to approach downed power lines — and had the good sense to keep their distance whenever they encountered them.

As the scene got more crowded and chaotic, Officer Littlejohn brought Gregory and Santa Paws over to his squad car. Gregory would rather have been able to keep an eye on his mother, but everyone else preferred the idea of his staying securely out of the way. But when Mr. Callahan finally arrived, Gregory jumped out of the squad car to meet him.

After hugging him fiercely, his father made only one remark to the effect of "Weren't you back at the house getting ready for bed the last time I saw you?" Then he hugged Gregory again, hugged Santa Paws for good measure, and rushed over to the cleared area near the station wagon.

The electric company had disconnected the transformers by now, and followed the other technical procedures for handling downed power lines. That gave the fire department an opportunity to move in and free Mrs. Callahan from the car. The dashboard and steering column were so badly crushed that they actually had to use the Jaws of Life to get her out. Gregory knew that all of the tools the firefighters used were designed to *help* people, but hearing the harsh sounds of metal rending and tearing apart was awful.

When the paramedics carefully moved her from the car to a gurney, Gregory saw several people quickly avert their eyes. That scared him, too. After all, emergency service workers were *accustomed* to seeing accident victims. Santa Paws was sitting on the seat next to him, and Gregory found himself clutching his dog for comfort. Santa Paws *liked* to be hugged, so he didn't mind at all.

Officer Nichols walked over and picked up her logbook. She stayed by the car to write notes, and Gregory could tell that she was doing it deliberately. Taking notes probably wasn't a top priority right now. Even though he didn't know her very well, he was glad that someone had come over to keep him company.

"Why did they all look away when they saw Mom?" he asked shakily.

Officer Nichols hesitated, as though she was debating whether to edit her response. "She'll be fine, but her leg is pretty badly broken, and sometimes that can be hard to look at."

Gregory immediately got a vivid image in his mind of a couple of terrible football injuries he had seen on television, and he shuddered. It was horrible to picture his *mother* looking like that.

"Can I go talk to her?" he asked. "Is it okay?"

Officer Nichols put her logbook down. "Sure. The EMTs are just making her comfortable right now." She caught the eye of the fire captain supervising the operation, and indicated Gregory. The fire captain nodded, and Officer Nichols opened Gregory's door.

"Stay, Santa Paws," Gregory said. With so many cars and trucks around, he didn't want his dog outside in the middle of all the confusion.

The dog wagged his tail, and sat down patiently to wait for him.

For a second, Gregory was afraid to look inside the back of the ambulance. But when he took a peek, he saw his mother bundled up in blankets, with a huge balloon splint around her left leg — and *smiling* at him.

"Give your mother a kiss before I have a couple of officers take you and Santa Paws home," Mr. Callahan said. He was grinning broadly, too, looking so relieved that he seemed about ten years younger than he had earlier that evening.

Gregory stared at him. "I can't go to the hospital?"

His father ruffled his hair, and then gave him another big hug. "It's three in the morning, Greg. Your mother and I want you to go home and get some rest."

Gregory would have preferred going along to the hospital, but he *was* really tired. Maybe even exhausted. He climbed up into the back of the ambulance, doing his best not to jar the gurney in any way.

"Hi, Mom," he said, feeling almost — shy.

His mother reached out and took his hand, holding on tightly. "Thank you," she said.

Now he felt *really* shy, somehow.

Mrs. Callahan winked at him. "Has Miranda been out pounding the pavement, too?"

Gregory relaxed then, and smiled back at her. "Yeah. Patricia assigned her the seawall patrol."

"You know, I wish I couldn't quite picture that," Mrs. Callahan said dryly.

The idea of plucky little Miranda toddling along the icy seawall above the crashing waves and rocks below *was* pretty daunting. The idea of Patricia *assigning* her to do it, was even more

168

so. "Are you okay, Mom?" he asked. "Your leg and all?"

"Oh, please," Mrs. Callahan dismissed that with a wave of her hand. "I've been through childbirth. *Twice.*" Then her voice softened. "Lucky for me."

Gregory ducked his head, a little embarrassed, but also very pleased.

"All right now." His mother pulled his hand over and gave it a light kiss. "I want you to go home, get some sleep, and *promise* not to worry. Okay?"

"Okay," Gregory said. He would certainly do his best — even about the worrying part.

Once the ambulance had left, with Mr. Callahan riding in the back, Gregory went to join Santa Paws. The dog leaned up to lick his face, and then curled up on the seat again. Officers Littlejohn and Nichols must have sensed how tired Gregory was, because they didn't try to engage him in much conversation on the way home. The only real sound was the windshield wipers squeaking as they swept fresh snow away with each pass.

"Um, thank you very much," Gregory said, when they pulled up in front of his house. "Can you thank all the other officers and firefighters and all?"

"Sure thing," Officer Nichols promised.

Gregory was surprised when both officers got

169

out of the car with him. "Um, I have Santa Paws with me. I'll be fine from here."

"Well, we're just going to hang out for a while," Officer Nichols said. "Keep an eye on things."

Now Gregory got it. This just might be their *assignment*. "You mean, until my parents get home."

"Something like that," Officer Littlejohn agreed.

The thought of having some adults around in case something *else* went wrong was kind of reassuring. Maybe it meant that Santa Paws would feel as though he could take it easy for a while, too.

"Okay," Gregory said. "Thanks."

When they got inside, Miranda and Rachel were still asleep, but Patricia was waiting tensely at the kitchen table. She had been using a flashlight to read her book about investing and — apparently — highlighting many sections. Gregory and the police officers gave her the whole story, speaking softly so that their voices wouldn't carry into the den. Patricia took it all in, asked a couple of pointed questions, and then stood up.

"Because of the power and all, we can't make you any coffee," she said to Officers Littlejohn and Nichols, "but would you like some cookies?"

The two police officers looked at each other. After all, they had had a long night, too.

"We would *love* some cookies," Officer Nichols said.

Once the officers were pleasantly occupied at the kitchen table, playing cards and eating cookies, Gregory and Patricia left the room to get ready for bed. Santa Paws wasn't so sure about having people he didn't know in the house, but since Gregory and Patricia didn't seem to mind, it must be okay. He followed them, wagging his tail and carrying a Milk-Bone.

The house was chilly, with the heat off, but at least there were plenty of blankets and sleeping bags. Gregory was about ready to fall asleep standing up, but they sat on the stairs to talk for a minute. Abigail meandered in from the den, where she had been sleeping at the bottom of Miranda's sleeping bag. She looked Gregory and Santa Paws over critically, twitched her tail once or twice, and went back to the den.

"Mom's really okay?" Patricia asked.

Gregory nodded. "Yeah. Dad was all smiling."

Patricia relaxed a little. If their father was happy, then everything must be all right. She gave Gregory's arm a small shove. "So, Mr. Hero. You *had* to go running outside in the middle of the storm like a big jerk?"

"Santa Paws was the hero," Gregory said. "I was just along for the ride."

Hearing his name, the dog looked up from his bone long enough to thump his tail against the floor.

"Anyway, you're just mad *you* didn't get to go," Gregory said.

Patricia grinned. "Yep. You've got that right."

Suddenly feeling exhausted, Gregory leaned forward to rest his head on his arms.

Since no one was around who might make fun of her for displaying affection towards a family member, Patricia patted him on the back.

"Come on," she said. "You need some sleep."

Gregory nodded, using the stair railing to pull himself up. "What time is it, anyway?"

Patricia looked at her watch. "Almost four." Then she remembered something. "Hey, Greg, you know what? It's Christmas Eve."

Gregory had to laugh when he realized that so far, this had been a *typical* Callahan holiday experience.

"So it is," he said.

Mr. Callahan came home around nine o'clock in the morning, with the news that Mrs. Callahan was feeling fine and would be able to come home either that afternoon, or early the next morning. He had fresh coffee for Officers Littlejohn and Nichols, and pints of cold milk and warm soup he

172

had gotten from the hospital for everyone else. Miranda thought this was the funniest thing she had ever seen.

"Soup, for *breakfast*?" she kept saying to Mr. Callahan. "You are so, *so* silly."

Officers Littlejohn and Nichols gave everyone cheery goodbyes and left to return to the police station. Officer Littlejohn *did* grab a few more cookies for the road.

Evelyn had emerged briefly from the linen closet to eat some catfood. Abigail joined her, but was far more interested in having some soup. So far, no one had shared with her, though. Santa Paws gobbled down his first can of food so quickly that Gregory opened another and gave him half. It was more than he usually ate in the morning, but after the night before, he was extra hungry!

Once Abigail was finished nibbling her meal, she sat down a foot away from the dog and gazed at him with her big yellow eyes. Being stared at like that made him very nervous, and that was why she always did it. Santa Paws kept glancing over in the hope that she would have lost interest, but so far, she hadn't even *blinked*. So he let out an unhappy little whine and took shelter behind Gregory's chair. Abigail's eyes gleamed with victory, and she helped herself to a bite of the food left in his dish.

"Very, *very* silly," Miranda said to herself.

Then she looked at Mr. Callahan seriously. "I like the party, but can I go home now?"

"Actually, we're going to keep having a Christmas slumber party *here*," Mr. Callahan answered. "Your father and mother are coming over here in a little while, and your mother will stay for a nice rest, while your father brings some more things from your house."

Miranda's expression was uncertain, and maybe slightly tearful, as she thought about all of that.

"It's going to be lots of fun," Mr. Callahan assured her. "We get to start celebrating Christmas a whole day early! Plus, it seems to me that *someone special* has a birthday today."

Miranda beamed about *that* particular concept. While she was occupied by playing with the crackers floating in her soup, Patricia leaned over to talk to her father quietly.

"Aunt Emily needs to stay off her feet, and Uncle Steve's going to be working a lot, so she's coming here?" she guessed.

Mr. Callahan nodded. "We can keep the sitting room pretty warm with the fireplace, and it's much better than her trying to run around after Miranda by herself."

Patricia grinned. "So *we'll* be running around after Miranda."

"Looks that way," Mr. Callahan said. "And as long as the pipes don't freeze, we're still in pretty good shape here, for cold water, at least. They've opened a shelter over at the high school, but I think we can avoid that."

"Why won't they let Mom come home right away?" Gregory asked.

"Well, they're not too excited about sending her back while the power's out," Mr. Callahan said, "but I think she'll talk them out of that pretty soon."

Gregory and Patricia sure *hoped* so.

The dog was ready to go outside now, and he scratched at the backdoor with his paw.

"Okay, boy," Gregory said. When he opened the door, he was amazed by the sight of their backyard. *"Wow."*

Patricia came over to join him. "What?" Then she stared, too. "Double wow."

"How bad is it?" Rachel asked.

"Looks like a bomb went off," Gregory said.

The storm was over, but it had left a great deal of damage behind! There were broken branches lying in every possible place, and a section from one of their other trees had sheared off. Part of the fence had fallen down, too. Long icicles hung from the roof, and every branch and tree glistened with its own coating of ice. The snow had been blown into uneven drifts, and their next-door neighbor's car was so heavily encased in ice that it seemed to be frozen to the ground!

The dog explored the yard to get used to the

new terrain. He had liked it *much* better before. He felt very ill at ease, and he moved around skittishly. All of his instincts seemed to be churned together into one big knot of anxiety. He just knew that Oceanport was a town *full* of problems today. He was tempted to run back inside and take shelter underneath Mr. Callahan's desk, but that wouldn't be right. People counted on him to help! But he could sense so much trouble, in so many different places, that he wasn't even sure where to *start*.

"Oh, no," Gregory said, when he saw his dog's rigid posture and fidgety pacing. "Santa Paws has that look."

Mr. Callahan sighed. "You'd better get him back indoors. We really don't want a repeat of yesterday."

Gregory yanked the door open, but his shoulders slumped as he saw Santa Paws gracefully hurdle the fence and race down the street in a blur of speed.

"What is it?" Patricia asked.

"There he goes again," Gregory said glumly.

The dog felt so conflicted about which problem to address first, that he stopped at the end of the street to think for a while. Who needed his help the *most*? Or, if he couldn't figure that out, who was the closest?

"Hello, Santa Paws," someone said. It was

Jane Yates, who he had helped a long time ago when she and her three children were temporarily homeless. Now they lived in a nice apartment, and Jane had a great job delivering the mail. In fact, that was what she was doing right now! It didn't matter that there had been a bad storm, and it was Christmas Eve — she was still going to complete her route. Her co-worker Rasheed was busy doing the same thing on the other side of town. It would take more than sleet, snow, and lethal ice to stop *them*.

The dog wagged his tail at her, even though he was distracted.

Jane always carried dog biscuits in her pocket to feed the many pets on her route. She took one out and handed it to him. "Here you go, little chum." Then she went merrily on her way.

Santa Paws crunched his bone while he pondered the possibilities. Then he heard an ominous rumbling sound, followed by a loud cry for help coming from a backyard down the block.

Yay! Now he knew what to do!

15

Santa Paws tore down the street, leaped over a stone wall, dodged past a fallen birch tree, and cut behind two houses. Finally, he found a man lying beneath a lot of wood! Oh, no! That looked *terrible*. The dog barked with great concern.

The man was Rabbi Gladstone, who presided at the Oceanport Synagogue. He had come outside to get some firewood to help heat his house. But when he pulled a couple of logs from his neatly-stacked woodpile, they were so icy that most of them toppled right on top of him!

"Good morning, Santa Paws," Rabbi Gladstone said, sounding a little winded, but very composed. "Could you get me some help, please?"

The dog whirled around and ran to the Gladstone's backdoor. Rabbi Gladstone's teenage daughter, Lisa, came out at once to see what was happening. She gasped and ran back into the house to get her mother.

The dog was perplexed when she left. But he returned to Rabbi Gladstone, and used his front paws to pry away as many logs as possible.

Drawn by the sound of the barking, Jane Yates had come running.

"Oh, no, look at that," she said in dismay. "Are you all right, Rabbi?"

"I think so," Rabbi Gladstone answered. "But, gosh, they're, um, really heavy."

Before pitching in to help Santa Paws remove the logs, Jane whipped out the cellphone from her coat pocket. She dialed 911 and reported the accident. The dispatcher — it was Eric, still on duty! — promised to have an ambulance and one of the ladder trucks from the fire department sent over at once.

When the paramedics arrived, the dog didn't recognize either of them, but they certainly knew who he was! They worked together with a squad of four firefighters to clear away the wood. The dog sat about twenty feet away, with Rabbi Gladstone's worried family and Jane.

Once the emergency service workers had freed Rabbi Gladstone, the only serious injury they could find was a badly crushed right hand. Other than that, he was mostly just bruised. But if he had been there for much longer, the pile might have shifted and caused much worse injuries. The paramedics bundled him into the ambulance for a trip to the Emergency Room. Just as the doors shut, Rabbi Gladstone waved at Santa Paws and shouted a quick "Thank you and Seasons Greetings!"

The dog barked back in a friendly way. Rabbi Gladstone was a nice man.

"That was good," Jane said, and handed Santa Paws another treat. "You're a good dog."

The dog wanted to be on his way, but it wouldn't do to waste a biscuit. *Ever*, under *any* circumstances. Once he was finished, he licked his chops. What a great aftertaste bones left! *Yum*. Then, with one last wag of his tail, he returned to the task — *many* tasks — at hand.

It was going to be a very full day!

Back at the Callahans' house, Gregory and Patricia were trying to talk their father into letting them go after Santa Paws.

"And what will Miranda be doing during all of this?" he asked them, since he was going back to the hospital to see if Mrs. Callahan could be discharged yet.

Just then, Rachel's mother arrived to pick her daughter up. She had been so pleased the night before when it was relayed to her from the police station that Rachel was staying with the Callahans. The highways from Boston were still not really passable, but she had been able to get on a commuter rail train that stopped in Oceanport, and took the town's one cab directly over to the Callahans' house.

"How many hours has it been since we've been able to get online?" Rachel asked, when she and Patricia were saying good-bye.

"At least fourteen," Patricia said, and shuddered. "Are you getting the shakes yet?"

Rachel nodded. "Total withdrawal. It's ugly."

During all of this, Abigail seized her opportunity to slink off to the living room. The door was shut to keep the cold out, but *that* was no problem for her. She easily forced it open by wrapping her front paws firmly around the knob. Then she scampered onto the section of tree lying on their floor, slipped out through the broken window, and went outside.

She needed to go join Santa Paws, and do him the favor of sharing her wise counsel and advice. How was he ever going to be able to save people *by himself*?

The dog was cruising up one street, and then down the next, pausing to sniff the air and listen for anything suspicious every block or two. Out of nowhere, Abigail suddenly appeared and jumped onto his back. The dog was so startled that he yelped and tried to shake her off. Abigail clung on stubbornly, and once the dog had calmed down, she batted him once across the back of the head to indicate her disapproval. Did he *always* have to overreact?

The dog promptly sat down, and Abigail slid right down his back and landed in a small heap in the middle of the street. The dog was amused by this, and used his paw to knock her playfully onto her side. Abigail was much *less* amused, so she hissed at him and rolled out of the way.

Suddenly remembering that he had things to do, the dog picked up his methodical patrol where he had left off. Abigail was welcome to join him, but she would have to keep up!

They covered a lot of ground, only having to pause for minor incidents. A man named Mr. Gustave had dropped his keys through a wide crack in his porch floor, and Santa Paws crawled under the house to retrieve them. Abigail sat on the porch swing the whole time, sneering at the notion of doing something as undignified as squirming around underneath a *house*. *She* would never dream of such a thing.

After that, they helped get Mr. Corcoran's cat, Matilda, down from a tree. She had run outside when he went out to get his mail, been horrified by the ice, and darted up into a tree to demonstrate her utter consternation. Santa Paws barked helpfully up at her, but Matilda only retreated two branches higher. Her footing was precarious with all of the ice, and now she was too afraid to go up *or* down.

182

Abigail observed all of this without much interest. But the cat's owner was very upset, so she grumpily climbed the tree herself. Santa Paws didn't like watching this, because he was afraid she might fall. Abigail jumped boldly from branch to branch until she was only a foot or two away from Matilda. Then she gave her a long, unblinking stare. Matilda stared back. They stared, and stared, and stared.

Finally, Abigail got so bored that she hissed and pretended that she was going to pounce on the other cat. Matilda was frightened enough to race down the tree and fling herself into the safety of Mr. Corcoran's arms.

"Thank you so much, Santa Paws," Mr. Corcoran said as he carried his adored pet back to the house. "And your friend, too!"

Abigail bounced around on the branch, enjoying the sensation of rocking. The dog barked sharply at her, but she paid no attention to him. Giving up on being able to get her to behave, the dog started down the street. Abigail scurried down the tree trunk and ran to catch up. She had been enjoying her game, but not enough to risk being left behind. She might miss something!

The dog could hear a cow bellowing somewhere in the distance. He tracked the sound to Meadowlark Way, and found a miserable black and white Holstein standing in the middle of the road. She had gotten separated from the rest of her herd during the storm, and now she wasn't sure what to do. Naturally, she hadn't been milked because of this, so her udders were swollen and she was very uncomfortable.

When she saw the dog and cat, she mooed pathetically and stamped her hooves on the icy road in frustration.

With one look at those sharp hooves and that big body, Abigail spun around. It was nice to hang out with Santa Paws, but she was no fool. A large, angry farm animal was *her* cue to go home — and stay there.

Besides, she was getting hungry. And it was nippy out.

The dog turned in time to see Abigail bound away in the general direction of the Callahans' house. He was somewhat disappointed that she had left, but now it would be easier for him to concentrate. Whenever he was around Abigail, he spent most of his time bracing for whatever awful thing she might do to him next.

He didn't want to get anywhere near those hooves, so he kept his distance as he herded the cow down the road towards the nearest farm. He knew where she lived, because he had brought home one or more of the Jorgensens' cows many times before. In fact, he had become an expert cow retriever!

When Santa Paws guided the cow back to the barn, Mortimer Jorgensen looked up.

"Yolanda!" he said. "It's for you!" Their water pump had frozen, so he was busy hauling buckets from the creek for the cows. The creek had frozen, too, but he had been able to break through the ice with a pitchfork.

Yolanda, a thin woman in a huge Eskimo parka, came lumbering out of the barn in heavy winter boots. Since she and Mortimer were taking turns using a generator with some of their farmer neighbors, she was milking many of the cows by hand. It was hard work, and the cows were so accustomed to their milking machines that they found the idea of being milked by an actual *person* rather primitive.

"Well, good for you, Santa Paws!" she said in a remarkably booming voice. "I wondered where our poor Jessica had gone."

He was good! How fun! The dog wagged his tail.

Then Daffodil, the Jorgensens' elderly Border collie, appeared in the barn doorway. She quickly took charge of the situation, and ushered Jessica into the stall where she belonged.

"Thank you, Santa Paws," Yolanda said. "Maybe you should run along over to Mark and Bill's farm now. They're missing a couple of cows, too. I'm sure you can find them."

The dog barked and trotted back out to the icy road.

"Find" and "cows" was a concept he understood perfectly!

Mrs. Callahan convinced the hospital to release her late that afternoon, and by then, Aunt Emily was at the house, too. They had all relocated to the sitting room, to gather around the fireplace. Mrs. Callahan would be able to convalesce on the couch, and since Aunt Emily was pretty short, she would be comfortable on the loveseat. Uncle Steve had brought over a couple of old Army cots, and Mr. Callahan had dragged an old roll-away bed down from the attic. Originally, Gregory and Patricia's grandparents had been planning to drive down from Vermont for the holiday, but because of the storm, they were now going to come for New Year's, instead. It was probably for the best, since the room would have been incredibly crowded.

When Mrs. Callahan got home, moving awkwardly on her new crutches, Patricia and Gregory had to be careful when they hugged her. She had broken one rib and cracked two others in the accident, and they didn't want to hurt her. But they were *so glad* that she was back!

Miranda was completely fascinated by the big white cast on Mrs. Callahan's leg. She immediately found some Magic Markers and began drawing on it.

"I am drawing *very nice* pictures," she informed Mrs. Callahan. "To make you feel better."

"Thank you," Mrs. Callahan said with a grin. "They look lovely, so far."

Since it was dark outside now, the only light in the room came from the fireplace, the dim glow of Aunt Emily's lantern, and flashlights. Mr. Callahan had set up an old transistor radio on the coffee table, so that they could get some news from the outside world. The reports were saying that more than 90% of the people in Oceanport were without power, and three quarters of the town had no telephone service, either. The power company was working to re-establish power at places like the hospital, first. Their spokesperson could not really estimate when the electricity would return elsewhere, because the damage was so extensive.

Patricia and Gregory had been allowed to take a brief walk outside earlier, to call for Santa Paws. He had never come, but about half an hour after they got home, they heard the living room door squeaking open. It was Abigail, returning from her adventures. She had been asleep in front of the fireplace ever since. Evelyn had come downstairs, too, and selected a strategic position on the couch, next to Mrs. Callahan.

Mr. Callahan had buried some of their food from the refrigerator outside in a snowbank, to try and keep it from spoiling. They were eating as much of the rest as they could, so that it wouldn't go to waste. Cooking boneless chicken breasts over the fire was beyond Mr. Callahan's abilities, but so far, he had been very successful with hotdogs and rolls. Only a couple had burned too badly to eat. His attempt at making scrambled eggs over the fire was best forgotten. And, of course, after supper, it would be time for Miranda's birthday cake! Uncle Steve had hidden it in a pantry cupboard earlier that day, along with a pile of gifts.

Patricia wanted to read, but it was hard to see in the flickering light. She and Gregory were playing cards, instead. Later, they were all going to play Monopoly — while figuring out a way to allow Miranda to participate. The only game she really knew was Candyland, and mostly, she just liked to toss the pieces around. She had spent most of the afternoon occupied by drawing pictures and telling long, involved stories to everyone.

"I'm just really worried about him," Gregory said to his father, for about the twentieth time.

A hotdog roll slid off Mr. Callahan's skewer and disappeared into the flames. He frowned and selected another. "I know, Greg. We'll go out on the patio later, and call him again."

The radio continued to drone on with storm updates in the background. These included statistics about how many motor vehicle accidents there had been, how many people had been hospitalized, where all of the Red Cross shelters were located, and a long series of safety tips for coping without power or heat. They also announced the football scores, which Gregory listened to with rapt attention.

Patricia was already tired of cards, jittery about not being able to use her computer or watch television, and just generally feeling rather cranky. "I think I would have been a very bad pioneer," she said. "Remember *The Long Winter*?" That was a book by Laura Ingalls Wilder, about surviving on the prairie during the 1800s. "When they were burning straw and eating wheat kernels and all? No, thank you."

"Why don't you listen to your Walkman?" Mrs. Callahan suggested. "That way, you can still feel reasonably modern."

"Oh, yeah!" Patricia rushed upstairs with her flashlight, returning with her Walkman and a stack of CDs.

"You going to share?" Gregory asked. His Walkman was broken, although he was hoping that there might be a new one among his Christmas presents.

"Maybe," Patricia said, lying down on her

sleeping bag to listen to John Coltrane. "If Miranda asks nicely."

"I am drawing," Miranda said sternly. "Please let me draw now."

The radio announcer said something with "Santa Paws" in the sentence, and they all looked up.

"And now, on the local front," he was saying. "There have been *numerous* Santa Paws sightings around town, as the legendary canine continues his usual practice of protecting the innocent. We now have a live report from our woman in the field, Margaret Saunders, about one of his latest exploits."

Margaret Saunders was a woman Santa Paws had been kind to long ago, when he was a stray. Back then, she had been recently widowed and miserable. Now she was newly engaged, working as a full-time reporter, and very happy.

The Callahans listened as Margaret breathlessly told about Santa Paws racing to the fire station to bring a truck back to the Nguyens' house only moments earlier. Apparently, a small fire had started when a candle tipped over, but Santa Paws had intervened before it could spread beyond the corner of one room. Margaret interviewed the grateful family at length, and then reported on the earlier incident, during which Santa Paws had helped free a man who had been locked in his garage overnight. The garage doors only worked with an electric door opener, and so, when the power went out, Mr. Garcia had been trapped. Santa Paws had brought Father Reilly over from the rectory, and the priest used a car jack to force the garage door open. Mr. Garcia was currently being treated at Oceanport Memorial Hospital for mild hypothermia.

"Sounds as though Santa Paws is having a busy day," Mr. Callahan remarked.

"At least we know where he is now," Patricia said, and paused. "Well — sort of."

"Please stay tuned to this station on your AM dial for further Santa Paws reports," Margaret, the reporter, said over the radio. "And if you can get to a telephone, please phone in your sightings. We want to bring you the very latest information about these thrilling events."

The Callahans would *definitely* be staying tuned in.

16

As the night wore on, the dog got more and more tired. He had been running around for hours, and his stomach was growling terribly. After he found Mr. Garcia, the man caught in his garage, Father Reilly had fixed a bowl of water for him, which made him feel somewhat better. But, he needed a snack! So he cruised by the public safety complex, where a group of firefighters was in the back room, gulping down some beef stew between alarms. They were eager to share a large portion with Santa Paws, and the dog wagged his tail the entire time he was eating. Except for the celery, the stew was delicious!

After his late supper, the dog felt much happier. The firefighters were smiling, too. Some hot food and a little bit of time to take it easy made all the difference.

"Go home now, Santa Paws," one of the firefighters, Karen Berringer, advised, when he trotted over to the exit. "I think you've done your share."

The dog barked pleasantly, and went out into the night.

"Merry Christmas, Santa Paws!" someone else shouted after him.

He *wanted* to go home — he hadn't seen his family *all day*! — but he knew he needed to take one last survey of the town before he could relax. So many people had needed help today, and he didn't want to leave anyone out!

The dog started at the far end of town, and slowly worked his way towards the ocean. Almost every block was dark, but he could easily pick out the houses which were still occupied. Mostly, families and neighbors seemed to be gathered together, waiting for the power to return. He was happy because he sensed almost no anxiety or anger. At worst, people seemed to be tired, or bored. He could tell that many others were *happy*, and enjoying the novelty of spending uninterrupted time together. Laughter and conversation filled the air.

There was singing coming from one house — it sounded like a lot of people! Maybe twenty! The dog stood outside in the ice and snow, and listened to the voices wistfully. The Callahans never really sang, but he was sure that they were talking quietly and laughing right now. He couldn't wait to go and join them! Frankly, he couldn't help wishing that Oceanport was even *smaller*.

There was lots of salt and sand on the roads now, and the dog walked on drifts of snow whenever possible. The salt just made his paws hurt too much. He had covered enough miles by now to make his paws hurt, anyway. He missed Abigail, but it was good that she had gone home, because he would probably be carrying her by now!

He finally reached the seawall right before dawn. It was still dark, but the skies were much lighter than they had been. He rested his front paws on the cold cement of the seawall and inhaled deeply. The ocean had a very strong briny smell, but he liked it. The sound of the waves rolling in and out was soothing, too.

He yawned widely and dropped onto all four paws. Finally! He had checked the entire town! He could go home! Yay!

The dog was too worn out to keep trotting, so he just walked. What fun it would be to have a nice, long nap! He was thinking about Milk-Bones — big ones, small ones, and beef-flavored ones — when a chill ran unexpectedly down his spine.

There was more trouble!

His first instinct took him down Larchmont Street, but he changed his mind and ran the other way. When he was tired, it was more difficult to guess correctly the first time. He turned up Acorn Lane, and *now* he knew he was right. There was something terrible going on inside the white house with red shutters. It belonged to Mr. and Mrs. Malone, who had four children, and Mrs. Malone's mother also lived there.

The dog barked repeatedly outside the front door. The house was full of people — seven, as far as he could tell, and a cat, too — so why didn't any of them come to let him in? As far as he could tell, they were very, *very* sick in some way, and maybe none of them wanted to get out of bed. Or maybe they *couldn't* get out of bed!

He could go find his friends in uniform, but he sensed that there wasn't enough time. He had to act *now*. Since no one had answered the front door, he ran around to the back and barked there, too. There was still no response. How could they not hear him when it was so quiet? He returned to the front of the house, but still, no one inside had stirred. They scarcely seemed to be breathing!

The dog was sure that there was no time to waste — not even enough time to try to wake up one of the neighbors. He would have to go inside on his own. The dog took a running start, and then plunged through the front picture window with a crash of shattering glass.

He landed on a thick carpet, which broke his

fall. He shook once to knock away as much glass as possible, and then looked around to locate the family. There was a bad smell inside the house that made him cough, and whenever he took a breath, he felt dizzy. This was not a good place to be!

The dog ran into the living room, barking at the top of his lungs. The whole family was sleeping in there, wrapped up in blankets or sleeping bags. No matter how fiercely he barked, not one of them moved. What was *wrong* with them?

There was a small child curled into a sleeping bag by his feet, and he dragged the bag — with the child still inside — into the front room by the open window. He was able to pull out two more children the same way, and then he carried the family cat by the scruff of the neck. All of the other people were heavy, and it would be hard to transport them.

Not sure what to do, he yanked the father off the couch. The father landed heavily on the floor and mumbled something garbled. The dog pawed at the man's chest, trying to rouse him. He felt so dizzy and sick himself now that it was an effort to stay conscious.

Hearing a voice out by the broken window, the dog went to see what the children were doing. The older girl seemed to be waking up and coughing a lot. Standing by the open window as the cold air and wind rushed in made the dog feel a little better, and it seemed to be helping the girl recover, too. Her name was Jill, and she was twelve. The other two children he had dragged out were Vicky and Owen, and they were eight-year-old twins.

"Santa Paws?" Jill asked dully.

The dog barked.

"What's — I don't — I — " She looked around in complete confusion.

The dog ran to the front door and barked again.

Jill lurched to her feet and went over to open the door for him. The dog quickly dragged Vicky and Owen's sleeping bags out to the porch. He carefully set the cat down next to them, then went back into the house.

"Is it a fire?" Jill asked, still sounding vague.

The dog returned to the living room and fastened his teeth firmly around the end of the oldest boy's sleeping bag. His name was Larry, and he was fourteen. Using every ounce of his strength, the dog hauled him out of the living room.

By now, Jill had grasped that there was something seriously wrong, and she helped Santa Paws get Larry outside. Then they both went back to get Jill's grandmother and parents.

"Mom? Dad? Gram? Wake up!" Jill shouted. "We have to get out!"

Her father tried to sit up, but slumped down again.

"Come on, Dad," Jill said, struggling to get him to his feet.

That gave the dog a chance to concentrate on helping the mother and grandmother. The grandmother felt sort of frail, and he was afraid to knock her off the mattress where she was sleeping. He grabbed the mother's nightgown sleeve with his jaw and tugged as hard as he could.

"Go back to sleep," she muttered.

The dog dragged her as far as the hall before her sleeve tore. So, he switched to the other sleeve and got her halfway into the living room. This was very strenuous!

Jill was helping her father outside, and her brother Larry had revived enough to be able to get his mother. In the meantime, the dog was in the living room, trying to figure out a way to help the grandmother. He was joined by Larry and Jill, who worked together to carry her to the porch.

Everyone was finally out! But it was so cold that the dog raced to the living room one last time to drag some blankets out to the stricken family.

While they sat groggily on the porch, he took off for the public safety complex. His legs didn't want to work right, and he stumbled every so often. He felt sick the way he had when he was stolen by bad, mean thieves who made him smell a handkerchief soaked in nasty drugs. This was terrible!

It took him longer than he expected, because his legs were so rubbery. But the fire and rescue personnel leaped up the second they saw him, and with the help of his paramedic friends, Fran and Saul, he was able to guide everyone back to the Malones' house.

The family had been using a kerosine heater to keep their house warm, but they had not ventilated it properly. So the house filled with fumes and — more dangerously — odorless carbon monoxide gas. If Santa Paws had not forced his way inside, the entire family would have suffocated in their sleep from lack of oxygen.

It took several ambulances to transfer all of them to the hospital for oxygen therapy. The family was doing better since they had spent time in the fresh air, but they still needed medical attention.

The sun had come up, and it looked as though it was going to be a beautiful day. Already, some of the ice was beginning to melt. While the firefighters worked on ventilating and fumigating the house, Santa Paws climbed slowly to his feet. He *really* needed a nap.

"Not so fast, Santa Paws," Saul said, and grabbed his collar. "You need a little help yourself." Then he fitted a mask over the dog's face so that he could inhale some pure oxygen, while Fran checked his vital signs.

The dog was impatient to get home, but the air he was breathing was making him feel so much stronger! He rested on a blanket in the back of an ambulance, inhaling deeply.

"We're going to drive you home, too," Fran said. "*You*, Santa Paws, are going to enjoy the rest of this holiday — and that's an order!"

The dog wagged his tail a few times.

"Home" was one of the very best words of all!

The Callahans were in their sitting room, opening Christmas gifts. Oceanport's traditional non-religious, interdenominational holiday service had been postponed for a few days, so that everyone in town would be able to attend. It felt strange not to be going to church on Christmas — and even stranger to be celebrating without Santa Paws. The radio had yet to report a sighting this morning! But the station *was* playing Christmas carols, which helped brighten the atmosphere.

"Where is Santa Paws?" Miranda asked. "It is very sad when he isn't here."

"I'm sure he'll be along, Miranda. He was working a long shift last night, too," Uncle Steve said, and handed her a brightly-wrapped gift. "Why don't you open this? I think Santa Claus picked it especially for you." Uncle Steve had come over to the house at about four in the morning, when his commanding officer finally forced him to take some time off.

Miranda tore off the wrapping paper and stared with great glee at a new Barbie doll. "Hooray for Santa Claus!" she said.

Gregory and Patricia were drinking the last of the orange juice, and eating a bizarre morning meal of boxed macaroni and cheese their father had cooked in a saucepan over the fire, plus a banana each, and some carrots. Abigail stole a carrot stick when no one was looking and was now batting it lazily from one paw to another. Their parents and Aunt Emily were eating unevenly heated chicken tetrazzini from the freezer, while Uncle Steve settled for a couple of hotdogs.

"Well, at least we didn't have to carve each other presents out of sticks or something," Patricia said.

Gregory grinned at her. "Not so fast. You haven't opened mine yet."

Mrs. Callahan looked thoughtful. "You know, in spite of everything, this has actually been one of our nicest Christmases ever. Instead of running around all over the place, we've just been spending time together. It's what Christmas is supposed to be, really."

"Okay," Mr. Callahan said, "but next year, in Jerusalem."

Mrs. Callahan and Aunt Emily both laughed.

"*Next* year I will get to play with the baby sister Mommy is giving me," Miranda said solemnly.

"What if it's a baby brother?" Aunt Emily asked.

"It will *not* be," Miranda said.

"Yeah, really," Patricia agreed. "Baby brothers are a big pain."

"Yeah, well, hope you like the comb I whittled you," Gregory said.

"I'm sure I will." Patricia reached into the pile of presents and tossed one to him. "Here, hope you like the necklace I made you out of dried leaves and beans."

Then they all heard a small truck pulling up outside, and saw a flashing red light through the open curtains.

"What is *that*?" Uncle Steve asked. He got up and looked out the window. "Well, it looks like we have company."

Gregory went to open the front door and saw — Santa Paws! He was hopping out of an ambulance, and two paramedics were right behind him.

The dog barked triumphantly and ran to jump on Gregory.

"Hey, boy, welcome home!" Gregory hugged him. "Merry Christmas!"

The dog barked again and rushed into the house to greet everyone else.

"Is he all right?" Mr. Callahan asked Fran and Saul.

"He's fine," Saul promised. "He was saving the Malones from carbon monoxide poisoning and he inhaled some himself. But he's had oxygen, and we stopped off at Dr. Kasanofsky's house on the way over here just to be sure." Dr. Kasanofsky was Santa Paws' veterinarian. "He said just to keep him quiet for a few days."

"And only walk him on a leash," Fran added.

Then she and Saul looked at each other.

"And *no more rescues* this week," they said together.

"Well, I think we can manage all of that," Mr. Callahan said. "Thank you for helping him."

When he invited the paramedics inside, they told him that it was time to go home and see *their* families. So, after a quick exchange of Merry Christmases and Happy Holidays, Saul and Fran left.

In the sitting room, Santa Paws ran to each person — or cat — in turn to jump on them, kiss them, and otherwise say hello. Everyone was overjoyed to see him, except for Abigail who yawned, and stretched, and went back to sleep. But she *did* allow herself a tiny, little purr — which the dog heard.

"Well, okay," Gregory said. "*Now* it feels like Christmas!"

The dog sat down with very straight posture and lifted one paw expectantly.

"How about a Milk-Bone?" Patricia suggested.

The dog barked noisily. Yes! That would be perfect! Patricia was *so smart*! He loved her! He loved *everyone*.

It was so nice to be together that they all sat quietly, and looked at one another fondly, and listened to the holiday music playing on the radio. It didn't even seem important to open any more of their presents. Being safe, and together, was all that mattered. Then, a radio announcer cut in, right in the middle of "O Come, All Ye Faithful."

"Ladies and gentlemen, we have a very special report," he said, sounding very excited. "We have had one final Santa Paws sighting! Our beloved local hero has just been spotted by one of our eagle-eyed reporters entering his house to rejoin his family. Welcome home, Santa Paws, and Merry Christmas, everyone!"

Mr. Callahan lifted his cup of somewhat warm coffee. "I'll second that."

The rest of the family nodded. How could any of them argue with *those* sentiments?

"We now return you to our regular scheduled programming," the radio announcer said, and then, "We Wish You a Merry Christmas" began to play.

Santa Paws wagged his tail and curled up on the rug between Abigail and Evelyn. Each cat reached out a paw and gave him a light pat before going back to sleep. That made the dog very happy, and looking down at his Milk-Bone made him even happier.

It was a great day!

'Tis the Season to Be Reading!

All titles: $4.50 US

Available wherever you buy books, or use this order form.

❑ BFH 0-439-21627-3 **The Santa Solution**
❑ BFH 0-439-12911-7 **Santa S.O.S.**
❑ BFH 0-590-37990-9 **Santa Paws**
❑ BFH 0-439-20849-1 **Santa Paws to the Rescue**

Scholastic Inc., P.O. Box 7502, Jefferson City, MO 65102

Please send me the books I have checked above. I am enclosing $_____ (please add $2.00 to cover shipping and handling). Send check or money order–no cash or C.O.D.s please.

Name_____Birth date_____

Address_____

City_____State/Zip_____

Please allow four to six weeks for delivery. Offer good in U.S.A. only. Sorry, mail orders are not available to residents of Canada. Prices subject to change.

SAN1000